Another Woman's Man

Carrie-Ann Schless

CROOKED
CAT

Discover us online:
www.crookedcatbooks.com

Join us on facebook:
www.facebook.com/crookedcat

Tweet a photo of yourself holding
this book to **@crookedcatbooks**
and something nice will happen.

To My Mum,
My Dad and
My Children.

For showing me
love is unconditional.

About the Author

Carrie-Ann lives in South East England with her three children, her cats and her dog with her mum just a short drive away. She is never bored. She fills her time with reading, writing, tv series binge watching, amateur dramatics, dog walks, dinner with friends, the park, taking her children to clubs and the odd glass or three of something alcoholic.

Carrie-Ann is a self confessed Social Media addict who can normally be found somewhere floating around the World Wide Web. However, learning to use it for marketing has been a trying experience. She would love you to get in touch by connecting to her on Facebook or on Twitter, Instagram, Snapchat and other sites. All can be found at **www.carrieannschless.com** as well as her blog.

Acknowledgements

I wish there was room here to give a mention to every person who has supported me on my road to publication. I love you and thank you all.

I would like to give a huge shout out to my good friend Claire, who enjoyed the silly story I showed her and encouraged me to turn it into this Novel. You made what would have been another forgotten scribble into what it is now. Thank you.

To my Musketeers, Louisa and Chanelle, for your constant words of support and building me back up every time I couldn't see the blue skies.

To all my other friends, for everything you have ever done for me. Especially Kelly, Katie and Brooke for being special Aunties to my children and putting that extra bit of love in their life.

My amazing friends at work for putting up with my constant

waffling about book progress and our hilarious nights out.

My Teacher – Mrs Bradley – who fanned my love of English. Thank you for still being here so many years on.

To mine and my children's family for believing in me and never doubting that I could achieve great things, and encouraging me to use my "talent". For helping to delete the doubt I usually have in myself.

To my Nan, I miss you and wish you could have seen me get published.

To my publishers, Laurence and Steph, for seeing something in my story and putting their faith in me. To my editor, Christine McPherson for her spectacular eye. Our Crooked Cat Authors Community for all their help and support – and might I add really improving my to be read list!

And finally to my Angels, just for being there.

Another
Woman's Man

Chapter One

The Oxford English Dictionary defines adultery as 'voluntary sex between a married person and a person who is not their spouse'. A married person. Perhaps I am wrong to be so black and white, but does that then mean a person who is not married cannot commit adultery? What happens when the man you lie with, or wish to, isn't actually married? No law is broken. No vow has been made. Have you actually done anything wrong?

I am not a bad person. Well, I like to think I'm not. I volunteer. I give to charities. I always like to pay my way. I have never bunked the train, or left a restaurant without leaving the correct tip. I only ever use my credit cards in real emergencies. That is, of course, if you call buying a pair of killer heels and matching handbag an emergency. Even so, I always pay my bills on time. I have never been late with my rent payments, utility bills or loan repayments. I have savings. I have a TV licence. I have a clean driving licence. Yes, that's right! I have never been pulled over for speeding or drink driving. In fact, I have never been speeding or drink driving.

Before I'd turned eighteen, I'd only tried one cigarette and one alcoholic drink. I hated both and vowed to never do either again. I do drink, on occasion. I am a typical 'young person'. I like to work hard and party harder. As for the cigarettes, I only tried smoking once more and still hated it. I am one of only two people in my friends' group who doesn't smoke.

Takeaways are a treat for me. I don't like to overindulge. I only eat chocolate on weekends, and always have my five-a-day. My body is a temple. A well marinated temple. I try to go to the gym at least twice a week, sometimes more, and my exercise dance DVD is done so often that I've just had to reorder it on Amazon as I've worn the disc out.

I visit my Nan every Sunday, and phone her on Tuesdays and Thursdays. Once a month, I drive her to visit Grandad's grave. She used to go by bus, but once she moved into the home she was on a different bus route and it took over an hour. We have a twenty-minute drive, replace flowers, say a prayer, and still have time for a cream tea on the way home. She looked after me when I was little and Mum was working, now it's my turn.

I have morals. I believe in rules. I would never steal. In fact, as a child I got caught shoplifting because I was taking back something the kids across the road had stolen for me! I believe in relationships. I believe love is love, no matter if it is between a man and a woman, or two men, or two women. I hate cheaters. If you love someone, why would you want to cheat on them? I have been approached by a few married men in the past and haven't thought twice about turning them down. I would never, ever touch another woman's man.

Until him.

Chapter Two

I was never looking for love; it kind of just happened. I was burned at a young age. Before my 17th birthday, I had already loved and lost. Funnily enough, even at that age I was traded in for a younger model. I loved Martin with all my heart. We had been friends all through school, but in our final year he suddenly went from trusty companion to all I'd ever wanted from life.

Yes, now when I look back I know I was naive. I think every girl has this fairytale idea that their first love will be their last love. We dream of weddings and honeymoons. I blame Disney! Giving us unachievable expectations of Prince Charmings on white horses, saving us from the evil witches of this world. In reality, they are all looking for someone younger, prettier, or just different. I swore I would never trust anybody with my heart again.

It was a few years before I even looked at anybody in 'that way'. I had a few meaningless one-night stands. They served their purpose, passed the time. Took Martin out of my head, for a few minutes at least. Unfortunately, Craig became more than a one-night stand. To him, I was the love of his life; to me, he was just a someone. Someone who wanted me. We dated for a few months, and I will admit I grew fond of him. He was nice. Kind. But there was no spark. I was still hung up on Martin.

I feel guilty to this day about how I treated Craig. In the end, I broke it off. I had to. I was still in love with someone else, and Craig was falling for me more each week. It wasn't a conversation I'd wanted to have. I missed the days at school where Lizzie would dump all my boyfriends for me. He took it well. Seemed to understand.

Two things happened that day. I set Craig free, but also set free a part of myself. I had let the rejection from Martin control my life for far too long.

Chapter Three

'We have needed this night out for far too long!' screeched Katrina, as we walked up to the heaving bar.

'I don't know if I can do this, Kat.' My stomach was churning. 'I haven't been out for so long. Can we go somewhere quieter?'

'No way!' She spun in front of me, nearly knocking me off my five-inch heels. 'You cannot blame anybody but yourself. You and Craig became hermits. It's about time you were out again.'

She was right. It had been too long. It had become harder to pretend in front of company that Craig was the one, so I found it easier to hide away. I was finding this difficult, celebrating my newly-single status, not because I was mourning the loss of a relationship but because I was ashamed of the way I had behaved the last few months.

My mind drifted off to Craig and his sad little face the last time I had seen him. I hadn't even cared, not really. Not deep down. After Martin, I had changed. I had become a horrible, selfish person. Uncaring. I hated that side of myself.

As we neared the pub, my shoulder was barged by a man walking faster than me.

'Sorry.' His head swung round to face me. I just smiled. His piercing blue eyes stunned me into silence. Wow. I felt strange all of a sudden. My stomach was flipping. As I stared after him, he disappeared into the crowd.

Suddenly, I wanted to race inside and find him. It was like Craig was gone and Martin had never existed.

'You ready?' Kat asked, digging in her bag to get her ID ready.

'More than ever.'

I took a deep breath and slipped into the bar.

As soon as we stepped inside, we bumped into Kat's usual crowd. I recognised some of the faces, but they were mainly strangers to me. I didn't mind. That is what you get for hiding yourself away. Kat did her introductions.

'This is the girl I've been telling you about.'

I felt a pang of guilt. There was me thinking I'd only been hurting myself, but I had let down my best friend as well.

Whilst attempting to learn their names and passing around how-I-met-Kat stories, I scanned the busy bar trying to spot the stranger who had caught my eye. Kat's boyfriend appeared by my side, handing me a vodka and coke.

'I hope I remembered right.'

'You know me, Sean, as long as it is alcoholic.'

We clinked drinks and laughed, then he leant to whisper in my ear. 'It's really good to see you out again.'

As the night went on, my hopes of spotting the dashing stranger wore thin. Perhaps I had imagined him. Maybe it was my hope personified; it could even have been the bottle of wine we'd had before coming out, which had acted as beer goggles and made him seem more attractive at first glance. As if I was going to find someone I liked on my first night out!

I was enjoying being there, but I didn't really have anything to talk about. I stood concentrating on my glass whilst Carly talked about her work colleagues, and Malcolm talked about his brother's promotion. Katrina was in a full-blown conversation with Talia about her upcoming wedding, and Sean was teasing Steve about the plans for his stag night. I wasn't really needed here. Noticing my drink needed replenishing, I slipped away to the bar.

Chapter Four

Taking a twenty out of my purse, I leant on the bar and prepared myself for a long wait. Holding it up to show I was waiting, I checked I was showing enough cleavage to get the male bartender's attention but not too much to piss off the females. Saturday night at the Crown and Anchor was the place to be. Live music and cheap drinks, what more could people want? It was in the middle of the high street, and of equal distance to the best nightclub in town and the finest kebab shop for miles.

I scanned around and noticed I was probably about fourth to be served. Being only 5ft 2, I'm usually pushed around in crowded places, but tonight I was feeling extra claustrophobic. I didn't need a drink. I needed fresh air. Tapping the shoulder of the leopard print dress to the side of me, I asked her to point me in the direction of the smoking area.

As I headed towards the door, I laughed at my own irony. I was actually going to a smoking area to get fresh air. Crazy, I know, but it was after eleven o'clock at night and I didn't want to be a victim of the Crown's one-in-one-out policy.

The smoking area was a fair size, as it was used as a beer garden during the summer months. Small clusters of rattan tables surrounding patio heaters were overhung with flower baskets and fairy lights. Pushing through the heavy double doors, I struggled to put my money back in my purse. As the air hit me, I felt drunk. It usually took me a lot, but maybe my nerves at being out had increased the alcohol's effect on my brain.

I found a place to sit, trying to avoid the clouds of smoke billowing above my head. Around me, different conversations blended into one as I tried to focus on my mobile phone, checking if I'd received a text. Nothing. I wasn't sure what I needed more. Water, food, or Kat.

Using both hands, I pushed myself up off the chair and staggered a couple of steps before remembering my handbag had been resting on my lap, and must have fallen to my feet. Walking back, I bent too quickly to retrieve my belongings. It was very Elle Woods, bend and snap, but the snap turned into a stumble and I fell straight onto someone's lap.

'Whoa there,' his voice cut through whilst his hands steadied me.

'Oh, my God, I'm so sorry.'

'Hey, no worries. You okay?'

I wasn't; I was mortified. I scrambled back to my feet, feeling instantly sober. How embarrassing. I turned, sweeping my hair out of my face, and came straight into contact with blue eyes.

'Well, I never ordered a lap dance,' he joked.

Feeling a little more confident, I managed a joke back. 'First one's free.'

'Oh. And what would another one cost me?'

'Oh, hunny,' I teased, leaning closer to him, 'you couldn't afford me.'

I placed the strap of my bag over my shoulder and spun on my heels. I felt amazing. I knew he'd be watching me, and prayed to God I didn't fall over again.

Making a beeline back to the bar, I found Katrina in mid-order.

'Where've you been? What do you want?'

'Anything, but make it strong.'

I needed to drink just enough to erase the memory of falling outside but not enough that I would repeat the experience.

After sinking our shots at the bar, we carried our drinks over to a booth near the front door.

'You managed to get seats. Great.'

'Thank Gemma!' Katrina giggled. 'A group of guys got chucked out for fighting, and she was in here faster than Usain Bolt at the Olympics.'

I guessed the blonde in the corner looking proud of herself was Gemma. She looked very young, or rather, looking at her made me feel old. As a very nearly twenty-one-year-old, the fresh face of a newly-turned eighteen-year-old stood out from the crowd.

Sean was looking around.

'What's wrong with you?' I asked.

'I'm looking out for my mate. I bumped into him in the Gents. Not seen him since college. I got him a beer.'

'Oooh, single by any chance?'

'As a matter of fact, yes.' Sean stood up and gestured over to a group of guys, while I got my compact out of my purse to check my lipstick hadn't rubbed off. 'Kat, this is Max.' Sean did the introductions as I rummaged through my handbag for my favourite lippy. I had five reds in my bag, but only one was the right shade.

Sean carried on around the table, reeling off names I hadn't bothered to learn, and as I replenished my lipstick I heard my name.

'We've met,' Max said. I frowned upwards; it was blue eyes. I smiled. I felt confident around him. An instant attraction, but I had a good feeling it was mutual.

'Hi.' I held up my hand for him to shake it. 'Shall I move up, or do you wanna sit on *my* lap this time?'

The rest of the evening flew by. I spent most of it talking to Max, swimming in his blue eyes as he told me stories about himself. Turns out, we'd grown up three roads away from each other. He was a few years older, but we knew some of the same people. He was friends with Nancy Parsons' older brother Jim, and I had dated his cousin's best friend at school.

The conversation and the drink were flowing, and I couldn't believe it when the taxi came to take us home.

'See you around.' I smiled at Max, kissing him goodbye on the cheek.

'I hope so.' He smiled back.

Chapter Five

Weeks passed before I saw Max again. It occurred to me, as I woke up on Kat's sofa, that I hadn't asked for his phone number. I hadn't even heard of Facebook at this point, so I didn't have the option of stalking through Sean's friends, or friends of friends, to find him. Every time we went out, I looked for Max, hoping to bump into him again. He was my last thought at night and first thought in the morning. I was obsessed. How could someone that I'd met just once have taken such a hold on me?

Exactly five weeks from the day I met him, I was leaving the gym when my phone started to ring. I normally ignored unknown numbers, but something told me to answer it.

'Casey, it's Max.'

My heart leapt into my throat. Butterflies turned somersaults in my stomach. I had to try and play it cool.

'Max, hi. How did you...'

'Get your number? Yeah, sorry, I just bumped into Sean and I asked him for it. Hope you don't mind.'

Mind? Not at all! If Kat wasn't my best friend, I would have kissed Sean then and there.

'Well, it would have been nice of him to ask, but sure, I think it's ok,' I joked.

'Great.' I pictured him beaming down the phone. 'Let me take you out.'

One date turned into two, then three, which then turned into weekends away and quickly evolved into meeting families. We became inseparable.

'He's perfect!' I'd say to Kat, and she would roll her eyes as she had heard it every day for months.

Kat and I had met up to talk. Max had told me he had

something very important to ask me. We had been dating for nearly a year now, so I was trying to prepare for what could be the big question and wanted Kat's thoughts.

But something wasn't right with her. The sparkle behind her eyes looked duller today.

'What's wrong?' I leant forward and placed my hand over hers.

'Nothing.' She moved her hand away and forced a smile. 'Do you reckon Max is going to propose?' She took a sip from her hot chocolate. Her comfort drink.

I had known Kat since I was four, and she was five. She was the year above me at school, but we were in the same groups for all our clubs. We liked the same things. ballet, tap, gymnastics, and swimming. The one day we had off from activities, our parents used to take us to the park. They became good friends, too, which was great for us. We practically spent all our free time together. She used to come and stay at Nan's at weekends, and her dad took us for ice creams once a week.

I stared at her face. 'Please tell me what's wrong.'

Her poker face crumbled away before my eyes, and the tears started to fall.

'It's Sean,' she wailed, barely holding herself together. I went cold. A million thoughts flew through my head.

'Kat, what about him? Is he hurt? What's happened?'

'He's cheating on me.'

I didn't think it was possible to hate someone instantly. My blood started to boil. How could he do this? How could he hurt my best friend? I saw red. I wanted him to suffer. Seeing my friend, my beautiful, thoughtful friend, crumble into a sad little girl, I wanted to cause him pain.

I had always looked out for Kat. Even though she was older, I had always acted like an older sister to her. When she had introduced me to Sean, I had warned him that if he ever broke her heart I would break him. Trying to stay calm, I comforted her. Hugged her, wiped away her tears.

It got worse. Not only was he a cheat, he was a serial cheater. Kat and Sean worked in the same hotel, where he was head chef and she was on reception. After working his way

13

through the chambermaids, he had apparently moved onto the kitchen porters. His secret only got out when one of them fell pregnant. In my head, I was ploughing him down in my car, when Kat threw herself down onto the table.

'I'm a laughing stock, Casey. How did I not see it? I can never go to work again.'

By the time we got back to her flat, Sean had gone. He'd taken everything he could fit in his car and scarpered. A pathetic note scribbled on the kitchen side said: *I'm sorry*.

They'd been together three years. They had been so happy. He was one of my best friends, too; how had I not seen he was a snake? I despised cheaters. To me, it was simple. You either love someone or you don't, and if you do you couldn't even look at someone else. I'd thought he loved Kat, I really did.

The rest of the afternoon was spent packing away any other signs of Sean. Kat didn't want them there. I helped her to apply for a transfer to a different hotel on the outskirts of town, and we packed her an overnight bag.

Stopping off at the Chinese and the off licence on the way back to mine, I sent a quick text to Max:

Sean's gone. Kat needs me. Sorry xxx

Chapter Six

Cuddled up on the sofa, smothered in blankets, we stuffed our faces with chicken balls and chow mein, washed down with the finest Smirnoff vodka, with proper full-fat coke. I'd let Kat choose the film, which was a bad decision. She chose *The Notebook*. In a way, it was good; the tears could fall all the way through, and she could pretend it was just the story. I knew it wasn't.

I cried, too. Partly because of the film, but mostly because I couldn't stop her pain. There was nothing I could do but be there. I had turned my phone off after sending Max the text, so I had no idea if he had replied. I had a quick vision of him sitting in the restaurant waiting for me. I hoped not, and uttered a silent prayer that he had got the text in plenty of time. But to be honest, he was far from my mind. I knew he would understand.

The four of us had become like a family over the past year. I suppose that was part of the problem. After my mum had moved away to New York with her new husband Jonathan, and my dad had retired to Cornwall, other than Nan, they were the only family I had. Sean running off was like losing a brother.

We swapped Chinese cartons for Ben and Jerry's, a tub and a spoon each.

'Do you think I'm a fool?' Kat whispered.

'No, darling,' I sighed. 'He is.'

The doorbell rang. Two short, three long. It was Max.

When I opened the door, he was standing there with a bottle of vodka, a massive bunch of flowers, and a sympathetic smile. 'Where is she?' he asked, handing me the bottle and sweeping into the flat. Crouching down onto the floor in front of Kat, he placed a hand on her cheek. 'I'm so sorry, darling. I

15

didn't know, I promise I didn't.' He passed her the flowers, kissed her on her other cheek, and then brought her into a massive bear hug. That there was the man I loved.

He gestured me over and brought me into the squeeze, which made Kat laugh for the first time that day. He released us from his grip, shouted at me to pour the drinks, and jumped to my DVD selection to find a comedy. We sandwiched her on the sofa and giggled the night away.

Kat slept in my bed that night; Max slept on the sofa. I held her as she cried herself to sleep. Rocking and shushing her. Once I knew she was asleep, I crept back into the living room to say goodnight to Max.

'I'm so sorry about tonight.' I slipped my arms around his neck.

'Don't say sorry. Kat comes first, I get that.'

'I love you.'

'I love you more.'

I yawned. I was emotionally exhausted.

'Get some sleep, baby.' He kissed me on my forehead. 'She's gonna need you more tomorrow.'

'How could he do that to her?'

'I really don't know, babe.'

I paused, deep in thought. 'What did you want to ask me?'

'What?' Max looked puzzled.

'Tonight at dinner. You wanted to ask me something important.'

Max rubbed my knee and looked to the floor. 'Now isn't the right time.'

'It's as good a time as any,' I pushed.

He looked as if the weight of the world was on his shoulders. He moved me round to sit on his lap.

'I got the promotion,' he told me.

'That's great news.' I was so relieved to finally hear some good news. Max took a deep breath. There was more.

'It means I have to move. Only to Brighton, but I wanted to ask you to move in with me. Now I can't.'

'Because you know I won't leave Kat.'

The realisation dawned on me. Sean hadn't just ruined

16

Kat's plans for life, but he had also thoroughly screwed up mine. Max wanted me to move in with him! This was huge. The next step in our relationship.

He'd been working towards this promotion since before we had met, so I knew he had to take it, but now I had a hard decision to make. I had to choose between living in a different town to my boyfriend, or my best friend.

Climbing back in beside Kat, I let a few tears of my own drip onto the pillow.

Chapter Seven

The sea was calm, with the sun shimmering on the surface. Seagulls floated on the breeze and tourists meandered along the promenade. A distant boom box blasted out old school songs, and fun and laughter was all around.

It wasn't a typical Sunday with Nanny Edna. The summer sun sent us to the beach instead of our usual café for cream teas. We'd spent a good half an hour cleaning and laying flowers at Granddad's grave. There were lilies and laughter as we shared memories about the silly things the old man used to do when he was alive. Remembering the good times was always easy, as there had been so many.

Back on the bench, with our 99s in hand, we sat staring into the blue whilst I filled her in on Kat's heartbreak and Max's promotion.

'So, are you going to move in with him?'

'How can I, Nan?' I thought of Kat.

'True. What do you young people say now? Sisters before misters?' I couldn't disguise the look of shock on my face. 'Sheila Hannigan's granddaughter has been teaching me the lingo,' Nan said proudly.

'Oh Nan! What am I going to do with you?'

She took my hand into hers, cupping it like a small creature she didn't want to escape.

'You have to think about yourself sometimes, darling. Katrina is a stronger person than you think.'

'I know.' I shrugged. 'But she's not the only person I have to leave, is she?' I hugged her close.

'You could always take me with you,' she giggled. 'I've always fancied Brighton.'

'I remember you and Granddad taking me there in the summer.'

'Good memories, huh?'

'The best.' We sat, silent for a while.

'I mean it, you know. I could look at homes over there. I've lived in Eastbourne my whole life. A change may be good.'

Back at Sunnydale, Nan had ordered me a roast beef dinner. The food there was lovely. Claire was a fabulous cook. Whilst pouring her gravy, Nan started telling everyone about the new life she was going to have in Brighton.

'Nothing is set in stone yet, Nan.' I took the gravy boat from her.

'Poppycock. Seize the day. Even if you decide not to go, I still might.'

Edna Parker was a stubborn woman. She got an idea in her head, and it stayed there. Nobody wanted her to leave, of course. They all started begging her to stay. I watched Nan, a smile on her face, loving the attention.

Soon it was time to leave, but not before a sing-song round the piano. After a few songs about apple trees, blue birds, and yellow ribbons, I said my goodbyes and climbed into my car.

Kat was still at mine, sitting on the sofa with my king-size duvet enveloping her. She quickly hid her phone. I could tell she had been crying.

'What are you up to?' I asked. 'You called him, didn't you?'

'His phone's off,' she sulked.

I headed to the kitchen, flicking the switch on the kettle. I got out two cups, two teabags, and a spoon. Taking a plate out of the cupboard, I called through to the living room and immediately started serving up last night's leftovers. 'Have you eaten?'

'No,' came the expected reply.

Placing the plate in the microwave, I turned it on then poured the boiled water onto the teabags. 'Multi-tasking like a pro,' I whispered under my breath.

Balancing the two mugs in one hand and the hot plate in the other, I rushed into the lounge and put them on top of a magazine on the coffee table.

'Pass it,' I said, holding my hand out for the phone.

Reluctantly, she passed it over. One hundred and thirty-four times she had tried to ring him. All unanswered. All went to answerphone. I dreaded to think of the messages she might have left.

I watched her as she forced herself to eat a forkful of rice. We both knew she would never get the chance to speak to him again.

'He's deleted his Facebook,' she eventually sighed. I had no idea what she was talking about, so she had to explain it to me. I pictured him as a serial conman, changing identities and moving towns every time he was caught out. Could we even be certain that Sean Hughes was, in fact, Sean Hughes?

After she had eaten some food and topped up on fluids, I ran Kat a candlelit bath with stress-relief Radox, and put my CD of old rat pack songs on low. It was our guilty pleasure; our favourite when we were feeling down.

After she had a long soak in the bath and I'd sorted out all the laundry for work, Max turned up and the three of us did face masks and played cards.

Kat's overnight stay extended to a fortnight. She didn't want to be alone in their home, so Max and I went there to collect post and extra things for her. A week into her stay, we finally dragged her out. She had barely left my flat.

Her work transfer had been accepted, so we went shopping for a new blouse. The one she had been wearing when she found out about Sean was tainted by that memory, so it just had to go. In its place, we found three white blouses, a black pencil skirt, a cardigan, a summer dress, two pairs of sandals in different colours, a little black dress, and a going-out coat. She bought new lipsticks in case Sean's germs were on the old ones, new underwear, new bedding, and a new handbag. Not bad for a day's work.

We had manicures, pedicures, facials, and booked in for a massage later in the week. Perfect.

That night, we went for drinks. I had texted ahead and warned her friends that tonight was a Sean-free zone. I wanted no pitying faces, no mention of how sorry they were. Kat felt shit enough without being reminded every five minutes. She was a trooper. I knew she would get through this, but if we could make it any easier for her I was sure as hell going to make sure we did.

Later that night, after dropping Max off home, the taxi took us to mine. Kat and I stumbled about, helping each other up the stairs. Max had already paid the fare – ever the gent – so all we had to worry about was getting up the stairs and finding the right key for the door.

'What a fabulous day,' Kat drunk-whispered, trying not to wake my neighbours, but speaking loud enough to wake up the neighbourhood. 'I almost forgot my ex is a cheating arsehole.'

'Good. That was the plan,' I said, wondering why my car key wasn't opening my front door.

'I love you, Casey Turner. You are the best friend I could ever have asked for. Promise you will never ever leave me.'

That sobering thought was enough to get us into the flat. Not yet, I thought to myself, but one day perhaps.

Chapter Eight

I really missed Kat when she moved back out. It was nice to be able to walk around naked and have full control of the TV, but I did miss her company. I'd enjoyed having someone to talk to in the evenings, to make me tea when I woke up, and generally to share the chores with. But there was one bonus to losing my houseguest. Sex. With or without my boyfriend.

My battery-operated one had been banished to the back of the bedroom drawer, and Max had given my sofa more attention than I'd had in the past couple weeks. The closest I'd got to a screaming orgasm was the cocktail. Spooning with Kat hadn't exactly been the same as messing up the covers with Max.

Morning, noon, and night. Whenever I wanted it, I got it. It was like being at the start of our relationship all over again. On the rare occasion we did sleep in our own beds, we had phone sex. I had never tried it before, but I figured it was worth a go.

With Max's move creeping up on us, I knew this would probably become the main basis of our relationship for God knows how long. It was so easy to say we would see each other every day and take it in turns driving to each other's houses, but when you factored in the time and petrol it takes I knew we would end up being limited to weekends and days off. The day he moved, I cried. Big, heavy teardrops dripped down my face. I honestly felt I would never see him again.

'Don't be silly.' He wiped my tears away. 'You're staying at mine this whole weekend.'

It was true. We'd had it planned for over a month; I'd had my weekend bag packed for a week, and it was already Wednesday. I wasn't sure if I could survive the next 60 hours, but Max was positive I could.

It flew by. His townhouse was amazing. Of course, I'd been and viewed it with him, but seeing it with all his stuff in it looked even better. I had my own room! Not to sleep in, but for my clothes. He had a games room, and there was a spare room for Kat when she came to stay. The garden was small, but with enough room for a BBQ and a seating area, and a cute window box with a colourful floral display. The kitchen diner was huge. Spacious. A more modern extension to the older part of the house, with a utility room where the old kitchen used to be. The living room was quaint and cosy, with a real fireplace and bay windows.

Every weekend that I stayed, I left a little bit more of my stuff behind. And a mere eight months after he moved in, I put my one-bedroom harbour flat up for rent and moved my entire world to be with the love of my life.

Kat had begun to move on. Sean was just a faded scar to her now. A war wound. She had just started seeing another guy. And Ben was as different to Sean as you could get.

Work saw me swapping Eastbourne's Arndale Centre for Brighton's Churchill Square. Although my uniform stayed the same, my surroundings and colleagues changed. It was sad leaving my retail warriors. On a plus side, it was slightly closer to the beach for lunch breaks, and I had different shops to browse in on rainy days.

And I loved date nights in Brighton. There were so many things to do. Cinema, bowling, rides on the pier. We had a huge choice of restaurants and bars.

Our Eastbourne friends would come over on weekends, and we would paint the town red, white, and blue. Sundays, Max and I would visit Nan together. She liked him. She'd decided against leaving. A new woman had moved into the home, and she was like the Thelma to Nan's Louise. The odd weekend I couldn't go, Kat went for me. Life was perfect.

Max would often meet me from work when he finished early, and we would go for a drink and a bite to eat. On this particular day, we went into a bar I'd never been to and which was quite close to Max's office. I didn't recognise a single face. Max seemed to know a few people, leaving me sitting at a table whilst he chatted in the smoking area about football results. I could see him through the window, obviously angry by his team's performance that afternoon.

Bored, I fiddled with a beer mat and looked around the public house. Old-fashioned patterned carpet, a jukebox over in the far corner, the flashing lights of the fruit machines to the side of the bar, and a pool table squeezed into the space near the window. I watched the players for a while, as the tubby guy in a grey t-shirt seven-balled a lanky, scruffy-haired bloke who seemed to insist on wearing his sunglasses indoors. This was probably their daily routine, playing winner-stays-on from end of work until kicking out time.

'Danny, you're up,' the chubby guy called out to thin air as he racked up the balls. I glanced over to where he'd turned his head but couldn't see anyone. Suddenly, the kitchen doors swung open and Danny's presence filled the room.

He looked smart, well dressed, but casual. A confident grin was the main feature to his otherwise plain face. He swaggered over to the pool table, gloating to his friend that he'd already beaten him five times that day. A pint for the winner. Bet a fiver he'll win. Heads and tails decided the other guy won the break and Danny stood back, chalking up his cue, sharing an in-joke with Lanky. I watched him walk around the table, line up his ball, and easily sink a red into the far corner pocket, with the white lining up perfectly for his next shot.

Using his cue to gesture, he started telling the chubby guy, Rick, his next few shots. He was sure of himself, cocky, but not arrogant. I found my eyes following him every time he moved. An elderly man walked up to the bar and Danny walked past me to serve him, taking him out of my eyeline. I took a sip of my drink and glanced over my shoulder. He chatted with the man, who was obviously a regular, called over to Rick to stop cheating as it was still his turn, and disappeared off to change a barrel.

Turning my attention back to the guys at the pool area, I heard Max talking to the man at the bar. He called over to me to ask if I needed topping up, and as I turned and said yes, Danny returned.

'Alright, mate.' He reached out to shake Max's hand. 'I didn't even know you were here.' They obviously knew each other. After a few minutes chatting, Max returned to the table with my drink and his replenished pint, and Danny went back to his game, easily beating Rick. We finished our drinks and left.

Walking to the bus stop, Max started telling me about his history with Danny. Max was born and bred in Brighton, and when he was at college he got a part time job in a nearby bar where Danny used to come in with his dad at weekends; merely a boy. As soon as he was old enough, he became the pot boy, then helped in the kitchen, and then finally joined Max behind the bar. They became The Lambs' dream team.

Danny had been full of ideas to bring in the punters. Cocktail nights, happy hours, live bands, and casino nights. He dreamed of owning his own bar in the city centre and wanted Max to come with him, but the bar work for him was just to pass the time and eventually Max got his dream job in Eastbourne, and left. When he returned for a drink just six months later, to catch up with his old team, Danny had left. Some sort of big fall-out with the landlord.

'I didn't see him again until I moved back. First day in my new job in my new office, we went to the closest bar for a pub lunch and there he was. Owning his own bar in the centre of the city.' Max looked like a proud big brother. 'I've only been in a few times, but I love seeing him. He reminds me of my roots.'

I didn't feel guilty for taking a shine to Danny. It wasn't unusual for me to notice another guy. Max and I were human. Of course, we found other people attractive; we were just never tempted to act on it. Max was the kind of guy who called barmaids darling and gave a wink as a thank you, but he loved me and I loved him. That was what was important. I could look back on this day and make it out to be something huge, but it wasn't. It was just a normal day with Max, and Danny was just a guy in a bar. He didn't even cross my mind until the next time I saw him.

Chapter Nine

'I'm getting married!' Kat screamed down the phone at me.

'Oh my God! Really?'

'Yes! Ben just proposed like a second ago, and the first thing I wanted to do was call you.'

I pictured Ben still on his knees in a restaurant, awaiting an official answer.

'That's great news, darling.' I couldn't mask the concern in my voice. I barely knew him. How could I be sure he was right for her? On the other hand, I would have trusted Sean with my life and look how disastrously that had turned out. Kat seemed happy; I didn't want to dampen that. We made the arrangements. Celebration drinks tomorrow night, Eastbourne town, sleepover.

The next night, as the train neared Eastbourne station, I rattled off my worries to Max. Kat and Ben had barely been together five minutes.

'Let's just enjoy tonight, babe. Ben seems alright, let's give him a chance.'

I knew Max was right, but I was really struggling living so far from Kat. I'd joined Facebook, Instagram, and Twitter, downloaded WhatsApp and Snapchat. We Facetimed at least every other day, but still I felt a million miles away.

Despite my worries, I had an amazing night. By the end of the evening, I was happy to hand my friend over to her fiancé. He was going to make an awesome husband to her, and drinking partner to me.

It was gone 4am when the four of us got back to Kat's flat. I fell off the sofa bed before Max even got in it. We were all in fits of giggles.

'I actually think my liver is begging me to have a weekend

off,' I said through laughter. Max went and made tea for everyone, and we put on stupid cartoons and drifted off one by one.

I woke up in the morning, desperate for the loo and with sunlight streaming on my face. Every morning after the night before, I lay still for a few minutes wondering if today would be the day my hangovers would kick in.

Once I knew I was safe, I made my way down the corridor to the toilet. As I neared the open door at the end of the hallway, I was frozen by the noises coming from behind the closed door in the middle. Oh my God, Kat and Ben were having sex. I tiptoed past their room, really wishing I had a much bigger bladder. Sitting on the loo trying to pee quietly, I put my fingers in my ears hoping to block out the sounds of his heavy breathing mixed with her murmurings of 'oh God' and 'yes yes, yes'. This was so embarrassing.

I then had a traumatic decision to make. Should I flush the toilet and let the amorous duo know someone was nearby? Deciding against it, I hurried back down the corridor and ran into the living room just as Max climbed off the sofa and headed towards the door I'd just come through.

'Morning, babe.'

'Where are you going?' I loud-whispered, grabbing his arm and stopping him.

'I need to pee.'

'No! You can't! Go outside,' I laughed.

'What? Why?'

'They're having sex,' I mouthed.

Max's eyes widened, and he listened down the corridor. I loved our level of maturity when it came to other people's sex lives. It turned us into giggling school children. He decided he would rather risk upsetting the neighbours than disturb them, so headed outside.

I made tea whilst Max started on his speciality fried breakfast. We hoped the smell of bacon would entice them out of the bedroom.

'Surely they can't still be going?' Max said, turning down the oven.

'Maybe that's why Kat is so keen to marry him.' We laughed as the living room door opened and a flushed-faced Kat walked in.

'Good morning,' she said.

'It is for some.' I grinned. Her eyes widened. She knew I knew.

'Alright, Casey, I'm sure we can be grown-ups here.'

'Where's Ben?' I asked, mock concern in my voice. 'Hey, Max, do you think she's killed him?'

Kat shoved me as she walked past. 'Shut up.'

'If she has, babe, he's sure to have a smile on his face.'

'He's taking a shower. Glad to see you guys are as mature as ever. City life hasn't changed you.'

'Oh Kat. I'm only jealous. It's a struggle to get Max to last past the ten-minute mark.'

'Oi!' I heard, as a wet tea towel flicked me on the arm. 'I last at least twelve.'

We always did this. Mocked each other in front of people, played down how much we had sex, but secretly behind closed doors we had never really left the honeymoon phase.

Max served up the plates as Ben walked in, and the four of us sat down to breakfast.

Chapter Ten

Christmas season rolled around, and our social calendars were filling up nicely. My works do, Max's works do, shopping dates with Kat, my mum's brief annual visit, a trip to see Dad, and Boxing Day with the future in-laws. Max and I were excited to be hosting our first Christmas together.

My works do was in a hotel. Christmas dinner and a disco, with a few bottles of wine on the table. Max's was a little more upmarket. A night in the casino. All drinks paid, dinner, entertainment, and a small amount of chips thrown in.

Max had been teaching me poker, and surprised me by signing us up to play. I was excited to be able to sit down and practise with the big boys. I was starting to learn Max's little tells. How he tapped his foot when waiting for a card, and stopped instantly the second he was saved. Also, the way he rubbed his chin twice when he was trying to bluff. With a room of strangers, I would enjoy the challenge.

The poker room was a mixture of people from the Christmas parties and walk-ins off the street. Max and I got seated on different tables. There were about seven women in a room of ninety. I was starting to feel nervous. Was I even ready for this? Playing strip poker with my boyfriend at home, and a bit of full tilt online, wasn't probably the best warm-up for poker in the room.

I smiled over to Max who was in the farthest corner. He gave me a thumbs-up to check I was ok, then started to mouth something at me.

'What?' I mouthed back

He was saying someone's here, but I couldn't quite make out who. Daddy? That made no sense.

'Hey.' A voice startled me to my left. Danny.

'Hey,' I replied, taken aback. Danny's here. That's what Max had been saying. We'd been back into his bar not long after the first time, and I'd been formally introduced.

'Guess this is my seat.' He raised his eyebrows, taking a seat two away from me.

'Looks like it is.'

There was still something about him. A pull. A vibe. I enjoyed being around him. He interested me. The conversation flowed easily on our table. Seven strangers and us. One of them asked if Danny was my boyfriend. We laughed. How absurd that someone would think that. Could other people see the connection that I felt?

I heard Max celebrating a win over on the far side of the room. 'No, that's my man.' I pointed him out. We had been together nearly three years, and I was still so proud to call him my boyfriend. I blew him a kiss from across the room. As I looked back to my table, Danny's head turned away quickly.

Every time I saw him, we got a little bit flirtier. It was completely innocent. Max was the one, but I enjoyed feeling wanted by another man. He fancied me, that much was obvious, but neither of us ever crossed the line. When I saw him out and about, he'd buy me a shot, or sell me a double for the price of a single when I went in his bar. Danny had become as much a friend of mine as he was to Max. When Max was away or working late, he'd send Danny round to look after me or keep me company. It was great. I could flirt endlessly knowing he would never make a pass at me. Safe flirting. That was the only thing I missed about my single days. Flirting had always been a sport for me, but nowadays you couldn't even say hi to a guy without them trying to get into your pants.

Back in the room, the numbers were dwindling and I was getting a good stack of chips in front of me. I was replaying some of the tips from my poker book in my head. Eighty percent of hands should be folded. Make strong bets, double the blind is more likely to scare people off. Danny and I got separated as the ten tables broke down to less and less. In the breaks, the three of us huddled in the smoking area, exchanging our bad beat stories.

I couldn't believe that I made it to the final table. For the first time that evening, I found myself seated at the same table as Max. He had a few more chips than me. Danny had been one of the last ones to bust out, and was standing behind Max's shoulder. A crowd of ex-players and some of the other casino guests started to gather. I kept my cool and managed to get down to the final three.

My hands were starting to sweat, and I could feel my eye start to twitch. The pressure was on. I really wanted to beat Max. We were a very competitive couple, whether it was race games on a console or a board game with friends; we both really wanted to win. I knew if he won now, I would never hear the end of it.

Danny was talking to a couple of the guys from Max's office. He knew them from the bar. I managed to beat the other guy with four of a kind over his two pairs. The river card was being kind to me tonight.

So, here we were, Max and I, heads up on my first ever real game of poker. The blinds were high and we were both folding most of our hands, so money was just passing back and forth between us. Our dealer worked fast, shuffling and dealing the cards with ease. Max won a couple of hands in a row, giving him a comfortable advantage with his stack. He was big blind, and I looked down at my ten and king of spades. I considered raising but I just met his blind.

The dealer turned the first three cards. Queen of spades, ten of diamonds, and two of clubs. That gave me a pair of tens and an extra spade. Max looked confident, but with the blinds how they were I wouldn't be able to last many more hands before my chips ran out. I was scared to move. I didn't touch my hair; I made sure I didn't blink too fast or too slow. I didn't want to give anything away.

The bets were made, and the turn card came out. Jack of spades. Oh my God. I was one card away from a royal flush. I played with my stack of chips in front of me, trying to look disappointed. Max put the minimum bet, and I paused a moment before raising him by 400. He watched me for a while. I hoped he would think I was bluffing, and it worked.

Max stared me straight in the eye.

'All in.' He pushed his chips into the middle. I could have folded and given him most of my chip stack, but I decided this was my last chance to make a difference in the game.

I had a few different outs, so I called. Max had more than me, so I had to win to stay in the game. I sat back and shrugged. 'All in.'

I gulped hard as the dealer placed a burn card down on the table. The crowd moved forward to see. Max turned over his ace and ten of hearts. He was winning so far. I needed a spade to win. My leg started to shake. I turned my cards over. I felt the whole room hold its breath as the river got revealed. The ace of spades. I couldn't believe it. I had a royal flush! I'd won the hand.

It left Max just enough for the next four blinds. He looked a bit gutted, but I could tell he was also proud. Two hands later, Max was forced to go all in with nothing but a pair of ducks to my pair of sixes, and the game was over. I was the winner.

'Beginner's luck,' Max joked, as we shook hands over the table.

'You're just sore you got beaten by a girl,' I laughed.

'Yep. This time you didn't even need to get your tits out.'

'OK. I reckon I joined that convo at the wrong time.' Danny handed us both a drink.

'Strip poker, mate,' Max explained.

Max put his arm around my shoulder. 'What do you say to collecting our winnings and hitting the black jack tables, babe?'

'I say, show me the way.'

The three of us gambled well into the early hours, before Danny got a cab home and we went upstairs to enjoy the room we'd booked.

Chapter Eleven

'You're losing weight.' My mother pulled and prodded at me.

'I'm not, Mum. I'm toning up. Max and I have joined the gym.'

'Do you moisturise?' She pulled my face to her. 'Your skin isn't getting any younger, you know.'

'Nice to see you, too, Mum. How was your flight?'

'Not bad. The usual. Jonathan booked me first class.'

'He's not joining you this time?'

'No. The witch snapped her fingers, as per. Oh, make me a tea, darling. I'm gasping.'

'Max is on it. So, how is his mum?'

'Evil. The sooner she croaks it, the better.'

'You can't say that, Mum.'

'Nonsense. I say it to her face. Evil old crone.'

I had never met Mrs Carrick, but you could tell by the way my mother spoke of her that there was no love lost between them. Jonathan was slightly younger than Mum, and Mrs Carrick held her solely responsible for robbing her of grandchildren. Jonathan had never wanted to be a father, but didn't have the balls to say that to his mother. The woman did sound like a bit of a dragon; not that my mother was any sort of angel.

'Here you go, Jill.' Max brought a tray of tea into the living room.

'Oh, thank you, my little stud muffin.' She looked Max up and down.

'He's taken, Mother.'

'Shame,' she sighed in great pantomime-style.

She'd always flirted with my boyfriends. 'Don't worry, Max,' I teased him, 'she doesn't bite.' I handed Max the bags and he ran them up to the spare room.

Mum looked at me with a warm smile. 'It's good to see you, baby.'

'You, too, Mum.'

I loved Jill McArthur with all my heart, although she had never been a conventional mum. She was an actress, touring the country with plays and pantomimes. When I was really little, Dad and I followed her round from place to place, living in hotels and B&Bs, as she chased the road to stardom. Once I hit school age, we stayed at home, Dad got a full-time job, and Nan and Grandad took over chief babysitting duties. It wasn't until I was seven that Mum decided to take a break and give the family life a go.

She found it hard being a housewife, though, and she and Dad realised the only thing they had in common was me. They divorced almost as quickly as they got married. It felt no different to me. I couldn't remember them being together, really. Mum went back on the road, and I went back to seeing her on birthdays and Christmases.

When she got a starring role in London's West End, I got to see her more often. I was thirteen, and Mum arranged tickets for my whole class to come and see her as Fantine in *Les Miserables*. They all told me how cool it was having a mum on stage, envious of me getting to hang backstage most weekends. But I was envious of them having their mums at home to cook them roast dinners on a Sunday, and read them stories when they were young. Don't get me wrong. I was proud of what she had achieved, and Dad did a great job bringing me up, but it wasn't the same.

Then along came Jonathan, the week of my sixteenth birthday. He was a director on Broadway, over from America on holiday. After meeting Mum, he ended up staying for three months before whisking her away to play Grizabella in *CATS*. New York was amazing. I went for a couple of weeks over my eighteenth birthday, and understood why she never came home. My mum the Broadway star.

After showing her around the house and venturing to the local cafe on the corner for a quick bite to eat, Mother took

34

herself off for a lie down, muttering about jet lag and the time difference, leaving Max and I alone with the gifts she'd got us from America, both of which we hated. She'd got me a copy of a self-help book, written and signed by her friend Mimi. Max had an unusually large amount of Hershey's chocolate.

I looked at the small pile of gold and red parcels under our Christmas tree.

'I dread to think what's in them.'

Max smirked, thinking back to the dreadful Christmas jumper she had got him last year. 'Your mum isn't the best gift-giver, is she?' he laughed.

'I've got a gift for you, if you want one early, that is.'

'Go on then.' He moved himself to face me better, bending one leg underneath him, his eyes closed, and held out his hands. I leant in, placed my hands on his shoulder to balance, and whispered in his ear, 'I'm pregnant.'

Max slowly opened his eyes and studied my face. His lips began to curl, and his eyes softened. 'Seriously?'

I nodded, my own smile creeping up my face. I'd done the test that morning when he was off collecting Mum from the airport.

From the time I had moved in with him, we had said what would be would be. We hadn't actively been trying for a baby, there were no ovulation tests or baby-making sessions written on the calendar, but we had both stopped taking our contraceptives. He was earning more than enough for us to live comfortably, and with my rent from the harbour flat coming in monthly and more than covering our mortgage, we were financially stable enough to start a family. My wages and the left-over from the rent went straight into a savings account to prepare for the next step of our life together. I kept some for myself, to buy what I wanted, of course.

From the moment I saw those two blue lines on the stick, I started dreaming up ways to tell Max, but as soon as I saw him there in front of me I had to tell him. Max held my face in his hands and kissed me hard.

'We are going to be a family.'

I cried happy tears as he rubbed his hand over my soon-to-be expanding belly. By my calculations, I was only about eight weeks, so we agreed not to tell anyone yet. We sat close on the sofa, talking in hushed voices about how excited we both were, until we heard the grandma-to-be's footsteps coming down the stairs.

The rest of Mum's stay was jam-packed, visiting friends, hosting dinner parties, days out with her and Nan. Max was my alcoholic drink stopper, expertly swapping my vodkas for cokes, and spilling my champagne after an odd sip. We used all the tricks in the book. I went on a 'detox' and could only drink water. I was on antibiotics. I was the designated driver.

I liked the fact that Max and I had a secret. After her five days were over, we loaded up the car, waved Mum off at the airport, and drove straight to Dad's.

'Welcome. Welcome. Come in. Come in. Let me take your bags.' Dad was excited to see us. Safe journey? How long did it take? Did your mother get off ok? The weather in Brighton. The same conversation starters Malcolm always used. When the guys started talking about sports, I made my excuses to go off to the bathroom and freshen up.

My dad's bathroom wasn't crammed with soaps and shampoos like mine. Along with the rest of his house, Dad kept his bathroom minimal. There was one liquid soap by the basin. One toothbrush and toothpaste in the holder. A shampoo, a shower gel, and a flannel at the side of the bath, and a razor and shaving foam on the windowsill.

The built-in bathroom cabinet was small and probably housed his prescription meds and umpteen packets of Nurofen, paracetamol, and cough syrups. Washing my hands, I smiled at the thought of bringing baby Hilton, my baby, here.

I started wondering how Dad would cope with the chaos of a small child. Would he freak out, or embrace the world of being a grandad? Stepping out onto the landing, I looked around at the framed pictures decorating the walls of the upper level of the house. Me at four, on my first day at school; me at seven, horse riding in Devon; me at nine, blowing out the candles on my cake. The photos continued down the stairs. Me and Dad in Spain; me and Dad with Big Ben in the background; me and Dad next to a plastic Loch Ness monster. It had always been just us. Where Mum had moved on and remarried, Dad never had. I had never even known him to have a girlfriend. He had loved my mum his whole life, and I knew part of him still did.

'Come on in, poppet. I've just made a pot of tea.'

'Ooh, I'm all teed out, Dad. Just a squash for me, if you have it'

I had gone right off tea recently. I couldn't even get through half a cup without having to run to the bathroom.

Dad's phone bleeped and vibrated on the kitchen table.

Dad didn't flinch.

'Dad, your phone,' I pointed out to him.

He reached into his top pocket to take out his glasses, and peered at the screen.

'Ah. It's George,' he announced.

I went to the cupboard to get my own glass now that Dad was distracted. 'What did he say?'

'Stopped at services. Coffee break. ETA fifteen hundred hours,' he read out from his Nokia.

I glanced at my watch. Two o'clock. 'So, they are only an hour away?'

Kat's dad, George, had been Dad's best friend for almost as long as Kat had been mine. We loved our annual get-together. I will never understand why Dad had to move so far away from us all, but it was nice to have a holiday destination on tap. We would spend the weekend together, ending in our very own Christmas Day, complete with Christmas dinner cooked by Dad, and followed by George's famous home-made, brandy-soaked Christmas pudding. Kat's mum never came, but chose this weekend to visit her sister, who George hated.

As his car pulled in behind mine, George beeped the horn. I loved the way my dad's face lit up when he knew his friend was here. I hadn't seen Kat properly for a few weeks, so I was excited, too. Max and Ben had been planning days out at the pub and whatnot, so they got straight on with that. The house was full of laughter and chatter well into the early hours.

Chapter Twelve

Two days before Christmas, Max and I went into Danny's bar to deliver his card and present. We hadn't actually seen him since the casino night. For some reason, he had gone off the radar.

'Hello, stranger,' Max said, strolling up to the bar.

'Alright, mate.' Danny beamed. 'Long time no see.'

'So,' I looked at his face, 'where have you been? Have we done something to upset you?'

'No, sorry, I've just been…' he paused, 'busy.' A smile crept up on his face.

'There's a girl.' Max pointed at him.

At that point, a leggy brunette walked behind the bar and helped herself to a drink out of the gun.

'Ah, you've got me,' Danny said to Max. He called over to the brunette, 'Hey, babe, come and meet some good friends of mine. Max, this is Erica.'

She walked over, flashed her dazzling pearly whites, and held her hand out to Max.

'It's so lovely to meet you. I was beginning to think you were Danny's imaginary friend.' The three of them laughed.

I hated her. I stood there watching them, with a horrible feeling washing over me. I managed to keep smiling, pretending I was happy to see this scene. Our friend had a girlfriend; this was good. It should be. Yay, we could go on double dates and I would have someone to talk girls' stuff with when the guys were busy with sports and stuff, but I had taken an instant dislike to this girl. What also didn't help was, after me watching Max tell her how nice it was to meet her, they introduced her to me. 'And this is Max's much better half, Casey.'

38

Erica slowly turned to look at me. I smiled a hi, but she wasn't smiling any more. She gave me a slow look up and down. I hated her even more. I could tell she just wasn't a girls' girl. She was looking at me as if I was something she had scraped off her shoe. This was classic hate at first sight, both ways.

Before I'd managed to give Max the 'I hate her' glaring look, he invited our friend and this thing he called a girlfriend round for dinner. I didn't know who I wanted to hurt more.

When it was time to leave, I stormed ahead of Max, not even holding the door open for him as I went through it. I was angry, I was annoyed, and I really didn't know why.

'Who the hell does she think she is?' I grumbled, as I opened the car door.

'Who?' Max looked confused.

'Her!' I gestured back to the bar before throwing myself down in the seat and slamming the door. Max got in. 'Did you see the way she looked at me?' I pulled my seatbelt hard and clicked it into place.

'She seemed alright to me.'

My eyes blazed. Max knew instantly he'd said the wrong thing.

'Alright?' I started the engine. 'Looking down her nose at me as if she thinks she's better than everyone.'

Max kept quiet. He knew better than to disagree.

'Of course you like her! Why wouldn't you? She's smiley and friendly, and nice to you. And, of course, she is. You have a penis. Women like that make me sick.' Of course he liked her with her pretty face and flirty nature; any guy would.

Even at this early stage in my pregnancy, I was struggling to handle my hormones. We drove the rest of the way home in silence. When we got in, Max started dinner and I went upstairs to run myself a bath. I needed to wash this feeling off.

Once I was feeling better, we had dinner on our laps then snuggled up on the sofa to watch a film. I fell asleep on his shoulder. The vile woman was as far from my mind as she could be.

Max stared at me, a disgusted look on his face. 'Look at

39

the state of you,' he practically growled at me. 'You should be ashamed of yourself.'

'Of what? What have I done?'

'You're disgusting.' He turned his back.

'Max, please.' I lunged forward and grabbed his shoulder, turning him around.

'Max who?' It was Danny's face. 'You don't need him, you have me.'

Voices surrounded me: 'slut', 'whore', 'bitch', 'tramp'. They got louder and thicker; I felt suffocated. I looked around at a crowd of faces circling. Kat; my mum; Danny; Erica; people from work. No Max. Where was Max? I wanted him. He would protect me.

I screamed out his name and woke with a start on the sofa. In the light from the hallway, I saw a note on the table:

Didn't want to disturb you.

I love you, babe.

See you in bed xxx

I pulled the blanket up to my chin. I felt cold. I was having the strangest dreams at the moment. The clock showed it was 4am. I wondered if it was even worth going to bed for a couple of hours, but at that moment all I wanted to do was be near Max.

Climbing into bed, I shuffled up behind him as close as I could get. The smell of his aftershave lingered. I stroked my hand down his arm. At that moment, I needed him, wanted him more than ever. I shuffled up the bed so I could kiss his neck, running my fingers through his hair, gently scraping my nails down his back. I felt him start to stir. My kisses got stronger, my longing more intense.

'Max,' I whispered in his ear, kissing down his neck and rubbing my hands down his chest.

'Mmmm?'

'Max.' He slowly opened his eyes. 'I want you.

Chapter Thirteen

After the first sober Christmas and New Year of my adult life, Max and I started preparing for our first baby scan. The night before, I could barely sleep. I'd seen hundreds of scan pictures before, and always had to tilt my head to try and make out the head and the tiny arms and legs, but this one was going to be mine. I couldn't wait to be able to tell people. There were only so many times you could make up reasons to be on antibiotics.

I was working until twelve, then Max was picking me up to go straight to the hospital. As I was preparing to leave, I quickly popped off to the toilets, knowing it was unlikely I would make it all the way to the hospital without an accident. My heart sank. I was bleeding. I felt instant dread. Rushing to the staff room without even washing my hands, I scrambled to open my locker and grab my keys and phone.

'Hi, this is Max. Sorry I can't...' Shit. I hung up. I knew he would be in the car park, so I grabbed my stuff and ran.

By the time I reached the lift, I was sobbing. What was wrong? Why was I bleeding? I was getting strange looks from people walking past, but I didn't care. When the lift doors opened and I saw Max, I crumbled.

Phoning the hospital, they told us to go straight to our appointment and not to A&E, as Max wanted to. In the waiting room, minutes felt like hours. We watched happy couples walk in and walk out, studying their pictures with awe. Max asked me for the hundredth time if I was ok, but I wasn't. I was petrified.

'Casey Turner!' My heart leapt into my mouth. I had been so excited this morning, now I just felt sick. I wanted to get up and go home. I didn't want to know. Holding Max's hand, we followed her into the room.

'Just lay on the couch, please.' She knew our situation. She had read the notes. She was friendly and trying to be reassuring. I knew there were loads of reasons I could be bleeding. I knew some people bled all the way through their pregnancies. I mean, I had watched *Eastenders* and Sonia had, and even though I knew it was a fictional programme, they base it on things that can happen in reality. There were multiple reasons I could be bleeding right now, but something just felt wrong.

Tucking blue tissue into the waistband of my trousers, she explained the gel would feel cold. The room fell silent as she studied the screen, expertly moving the wand over my abdomen. She pushed in harder in some places. Max's grip on my hand got tighter.

I was waiting for that moment they showed you in films, where the tension is broken by the sonographer swinging the screen around and boldly stating they had found the heartbeat. But it never came. After far too long, she gave up trying. She turned to us with sadness in her eyes and said, 'I'm so sorry. I can't find a heartbeat.'

I couldn't tell you what happened after that. I could hear voices in the background. They were far away. Distant. There was another man there; a doctor, perhaps. I'm guessing Max asked questions and the man gave answers. Either way, I left that room without a single clue of what was going on. I felt like I was in a daydream.

Maybe I was in one of my vivid dreams. A nightmare. I didn't know I'd had a big decision to make. I didn't know that with just a single nod to the head I had agreed to take a pill to help speed up the miscarriage, instead of having an operation to remove it. It was already happening, they were sure of that. I just had to wait for it to pass. Max rang my boss to explain that I wouldn't be in for the rest of the week, then his boss with the same message. I wanted him to go back to work. I wanted him to leave me alone. I wanted to cry. I wanted to sob my heart out, drown in my tears. I didn't want to stay strong. I knew he was losing this baby, too, but it was *me* laying on the couch cramping, it was *me* bleeding heavily, it was *my* body rejecting our child.

I was letting Max down. I felt like if I cried he would want to comfort me, and comfort was the last thing I deserved. He didn't go back to work; instead, he hugged me whilst I cried, he replaced my hot water bottle, rubbed my feet, ran me a bath, and did everything he could do to help me through this time. He was my rock, but who was comforting him? He was feeling guilty, too. Guilty he couldn't go through the pain. Guilty he couldn't help me.

By the end of the week, it was over. I went back to work; party animal at weekends. Max and I went back to being just us. We didn't talk about the future, we didn't think about the past. We just lived in the moment.

But one thing never went back to normal. The way Max looked at me. He saw me differently, fragile. I put on a brave face, even to him. I was mourning something I had never seen. I left my tears until bath time, hiding my sobs with the running water.

I can't tell you exactly when it happened, but something broke in us. That perfect couple we had been, had disappeared. It may have been this first miscarriage, or maybe the second one I had six months later. It could have been the ectopic pregnancy I had the following year that resulted in me having surgery to remove one of my tubes. It could have been Max's testicular cancer scare, or the news that Nan had passed away. Every one of these moments mounted up, and put an end to our dream of being a happy family.

Eventually, I moved back to my harbour flat, and Max became just one more name on a long list of exes. It was sad, and it was unexpected by everyone we knew, but it was over... and I had to learn how to be just me again.

Chapter Fourteen

One of the negative parts of being newly single was being maid of honour to possibly one of the happiest brides in the universe. Sadly, their longest engagement on record had been made even longer by Ben being made redundant and a close family member becoming ill, but that didn't stop Kat planning her big day. Weekends were taken up with trying on dresses, visiting cake-makers, touring wedding fairs around the county, and making plans for the numerous hen nights we wanted.

'If I have to wait, I might as well wait in style,' Kat would say with a grin, as we searched the internet for fun and interesting things to do.

Since moving back to Eastbourne, I hadn't been working. I couldn't face going back to my old place of work; it felt like I was going backwards when everybody else around me was going forwards. I felt lost, but I was grateful I had my savings to give me time to rethink my life. I missed my parents, I missed my Nan, but most of all I missed Max. I did well keeping my brave face on during the day when people were about, but at night when the screaming silence of my empty flat couldn't be drowned out by my TV, I started to think.

I thought about how old our children would have been, if I had been able to carry them. I wondered if they would have been little princesses, or perhaps a little prince. I thought about how good a dad Max would have been, and wondered if we would have disagreed on how to discipline them. Then the tears would fall, and I thought about how I couldn't give Max the family he wanted. I thought about how much I had let him down, and how I had pushed him away. I thought about how I hadn't even put up a fight when he told me it wasn't working.

He deserved the chance to find someone who could give

him the family he wanted. I thought about how I died a little more inside the day I closed the door to our home and posted my key through the letterbox. Once there were no more tears left to cry, I would fall asleep on the couch and dream that everything was ok. In my dreams every night, we would have the perfect relationship, the perfect family. And then every morning, I would crash down to reality and relive that heartache over and over again.

One weekend, I had agreed to meet Kat in town to go over the plans of the spa weekend I was planning; hen night number one of four. She was working, so I said I would get the bus in and she would give me a lift home, as my car was having work done in the garage.

I was having a particularly bad day; it would have been Max's and my anniversary. Well, one of them. We had celebrated them all. First time we met, first date, first kiss. This particular anniversary was of the first time we had made love. I used to laugh about that phrase. People saying they wanted to make love to you. It had always been just sex, a shag, a hard fuck. Love couldn't have been further from it.

With Max, though, it was different. I finally knew what they meant. The intensity, the passion. When we entwined, it was physically impossible for two people to become any closer.

Standing at the bus stop, I closed my eyes, remembering my first orgasm, how it felt as it surged through me. How he expertly manoeuvred me around the bed, changing positions and taking control. I remembered everything about the first time.

Then I thought about the last time. You never know when you are doing something for the last time, but there was a small part of me that had sensed it. We had still been making love, but with an undertone of sadness that hadn't been there before.

A tear trickled down my cheek. We had never stopped loving each other, but sometimes life just gets in the way. One tear turned to two, then three, and before I knew it thick salty tears were flowing down my face. People at the bus stop were looking at me. I tried discreetly wiping my tears with the edge of the sleeve of my beige coat, but that just put big black mascara marks on it and probably smudged my mascara down my face.

As the bus pulled up, I managed to pull myself together a bit, sliding out my mirrored Superdrug card from my phone case to check the damage. It wasn't too bad; my eyes were red and I had a little black under both eyes, but it wasn't as bad as it could have been.

Stepping onto the bus, I placed my five-pound note onto the little yellow tray. The driver was looking at me strangely, probably noticing I had been crying, so I just said to him 'town centre'. Nothing happened. He kept looking at me, and I started to feel uncomfortable.

'Single?' he asked.

I was taken aback. Was it that obvious? In my fragile state, I suddenly felt angry. How dare he just assume.

'So? What has it got to do with you? So what, if I'm single? There is nothing wrong with it. Yes, I am at the age where all my friends are getting married and having children, and here's little old me, newly single after seven years. See, I'm not some sad single girl who can't even get a boyfriend. Just sometimes things don't work, and how would you feel if your relationship status was questioned every time a customer got on?

'How dare you?' I ranted. 'How could you just assume I'm single because I'm crying? It could have been something else. My dog could have just died. Not that I have a dog, but you don't know that.'

The bus driver was staring at me with his mouth open, but I kept going. 'I'm just trying to get on with my life and get back to normal, and if I have people like you throwing it in my face every day, how the hell am I supposed to move on?'

The driver shuffled slightly in his seat, hand still poised over the ticket machine. He lowered his voice, leant in towards me, and said just two words.

'Or return?'

I was mortified. I stared at him with wide eyes. He gave

me a sympathetic smile.

'Erm,' I started, gulping hard, 'single.' It was barely a whisper. Taking my ticket and my change, I sank into the first available seat. I had made such a fool out of myself, I just wanted to go home. I sat staring at my shoes the entire journey.

Sitting in the middle of Wetherspoons, Kat was in hysterics when I related the incident.

'It's not funny, Kat. I'm a wreck. It's like I've forgotten how to function like a normal human being. I miss Max.'

'I know you do, darling. If it makes you feel any better, he looks awful.'

I frowned at her. 'What do you mean?'

Kat looked awkward. 'We saw him.'

'We?'

'Ben and I.'

'When, Kat? Why didn't you say?'

'Because,' she paused, 'I knew you would ask questions.'

'Why would I ask questions?'

'You're asking questions now.'

'I'm only asking questions because you didn't tell me. That's the sort of thing you normally would. You phoned me the second you saw Craig in town when we had split, and you even told me you had seen Tom months after we broke up. I just don't understand. I mean, the only possible reason for you to not tell me is,' I paused as reality hit me, 'if he was with someone.' This wasn't a question; it was a statement.

'Max is with someone.' I was mainly saying that for myself, as if hearing it out loud a second time would make it sink in.

Kat studied my face before speaking. She knew me as well as I knew her, and realised I was setting into attack mode.

'I'm sorry.'

I shrugged. 'It's not your fault.'

We both knew I didn't mean that at this moment. We also knew I didn't really think it was her fault, but I was angry and she was here.

Nevertheless, Kat was trying to make it better; it just didn't work.

'I didn't know how to tell you.'

'Well, Kat, there is a magic little thing these days called communication. It's what people do. It happens in many different ways. In fact, we are doing it now; look, we are talking.' I was talking to her like she was an idiot, and I hated myself for doing so. 'Other methods are letters, postcards, emails, texts, instant messages. Etc, etc. Kat, you had plenty of ways to tell me, but you just chose not to.' And I stormed off to the toilet.

What was I doing? Why was I being so cruel to Kat? She was just looking out for me, being a good friend. This was classic shooting the messenger. Of course, she would have told me when the time had been right; in fact, she just had! I hadn't seen her properly this week, and what sort of friend would have text through that sort of information?

I got my phone out of my pocket and opened my Facebook app. Scanning down my newsfeed for anything interesting. I wanted to see his name, but it wasn't there. I pressed search, and his face popped up as soon as I pressed the M on my touch screen. Just his face. Gone was the picture of us on holiday in Greece that had been his profile picture for years. He had changed it before I moved out, but it still felt weird.

I clicked on his name, and up sprung his profile. His cover photo was a picture from a lads' weekend in Amsterdam, one of his friend's stag weekends. I half smiled remembering the story he had told me of him and Danny going the wrong way in the red-light district.

Slowly moving down his page, I felt cold. 'Lisa Parsons has tagged Max Hilton in a picture.' I didn't know the name. I'd never seen her face before, but there she was, the new girl in Max's life. She was blonde and pretty with a perfect smile, but that wasn't what bothered me. It wasn't even the pose, them leaning forward towards each other, two spoons dangling over a huge ice-cream.

I wasn't even bothered in the slightest that they were in my favourite restaurant, sharing my favourite pudding. What upset me was Max's face. He was smiling. A real smile all the way up to his eyes. My tears stung. He was happy.

The door opened behind me, and Kat stood there.

'You ok?' she asked.

'I need to get over him, Kat.'

'I know.'

'Did he really look terrible?'

She laughed and moved towards me, putting her arms around me. 'Oh, the worst.'

We hugged for a minute, laughing at ourselves.

'I'm so sorry, Kat.'

Shoving me, she said, 'Shut up,' before linking my arm and pushing me towards the door. 'It's your round.'

Just like that, all was forgiven. Kat left her car in town and we got a taxi home. I vowed never to take the bus again.

Chapter Fifteen

A few weeks passed, and Max's relationship status became official. It was announced on Facebook. He had phoned me in advance to warn me. We were still friends; well, we were trying to be. I still had to stop myself from saying 'love you' at the end of every phone call. I decided if Max could move on with his life, then so could I. It was time for me to get a job.

I went through all the local papers and the Friday ads, went into all the shops in town, and searched the internet. I sat in the middle of my living room, surrounded by job applications and copies of my CV. Handwriting each envelope, I had a pile to be stamped and another for me to hand deliver. My phone on the floor to my right kept buzzing with Facebook notifications; I had put it on vibrate to try and avoid the distraction, but it wasn't working.

The blinking blue light kept tempting me to see what interesting things it had in store for me. I was addicted. Kat had tagged me in a post, Quote of the Day's picture: 'Fake it 'til you make it.'

I smiled and quickly commented, 'I never fake it, baby! xx'

An inbox message instantly popped up, with Kat's profile picture in a bubble on the top right-hand side.

Kat - *What are you doing on fb?! Put your phone down, woman! I'm gonna be there in less than 2 hrs and I xpect u to be finished x*

Me - *Then stop tagging me in stuff! I'm soooo bored :(xxx*

Kat - *Ha ha. It will be worth it, babe. Ready to paint the town red tonight? xx*

Me - *No! I don't even know what to wear. Heeeeeelp xxx*

Kat - *Get back to work. Gotta go, big boss walked in. Love ya x x x*

I opened my other chats and started scrolling down. Talking to someone was a nice distraction but the question was who to message. A name suddenly popped into my head. Danny. I hadn't spoken to him in ages.

I searched his name and a similar bubble to Kat's popped up. This one made my stomach turn. A picture of Danny and her – Erica – kissing on a dance floor somewhere. 'Yuck!' I said out loud.

It suddenly dawned on me that Danny and I had never spoken on Facebook before. We had texted, phoned a few times, but never 'chatted'. I had absolutely no idea why I wanted to talk to him, or what I wanted to say. Considering putting the phone down and carrying on stuffing envelopes, I drummed my nails on the back of my phone case as my thumb from my other hand typed something and pressed send before I had really thought about it.

Me - *Hey x*

As soon as I had sent it, I instantly regretted it. Hey? Hey! What sort of idiot actually used that as a first message to someone they hadn't spoken to for months. I tried to think of something else to write that didn't make me look like a dunce. Like, hey, how are you? Or hey, what have you been up to? But no, I had now left it too long, so I put the phone back down and turned my mind to the job in front of me.

A few minutes later, something flashed in the corner of my eye. A little yellow light flickered on and off, replacing the blue one from before. I knew this indicated a Facebook message. I guessed Kat's boss had left the lobby. Unlocking my phone, I was shocked to discover a reply from Danny. So soon!

Danny - *Well, hello stranger! How long has it been? Too long, if you ask me. How are you both? Tell that man of yours to ring me x*

I just stared at my phone for a while. How could Danny not know?

Me - *I'm guessing you haven't heard then x*

51

Danny - *Heard what? x*

I wanted Danny to know. I needed him to know, but I didn't want to be the one to tell him.

Me - *About me and Max xx*

He might have guessed. He should have guessed, but along came the expected reply.

Danny - *What about you guys? Everything ok? x*

Me - *We broke up x*

I sat there staring at my screen... but nothing. I kept rereading the last line I'd sent him. We broke up. It still didn't feel real. After a good five minutes, Danny replied. I had expected him to be shocked. Expected him to ask questions, but the only reply he sent was:

Danny - *Oh*

That was it. Two little letters. O. H. Oh. Was that all he had to say? This made my 'hey' look totally acceptable. I started to wonder what exactly I had wanted him to say. What could he say? Another message came through.

Danny - *I'm sorry. I really don't know what to say x*

I laughed. That made two of us.

Me - *That's ok. What really can you say? I'm just surprised you didn't know x*

Danny - *Me too! x*

- *How long?*

Me - *erm... about five months ha ha x*

Danny - *Oh. That's awkward. Do you reckon you guys will sort it out? x*

Me - *Probably not. I reckon Lisa will have a thing or two to say about that x*

Danny - *Who the fuck's Lisa??? Lol x*

Me - *His new gf! Lol x*

Danny - *Girlfriend?!?! OMG, where the hell have I been?? x*

Me - *I know! Talk about being out of touch. Did you move to Mars or something?*

Danny - *Something like that. Just been working loads and stuff x*

I started stuffing envelopes between conversations. Time

was counting down, and Kat would be fuming if I wasn't finished.

Me - *So what else have you been up to? Other than work, of course x*

Danny - *Seriously nothing. My life has got boring. Where you living now?*

Me - *Back in Eastbourne*

Danny - *Ahh. Wondered why you hadn't been in.*

Me - *Ha ha, bit far to travel I'm afraid, though I am missing the free drinks x*

Danny - *You know you're always welcome xx*

Me - *I know :) So, I'm guessing Max hasn't been in x*

Danny - *Nah, not seen him x*

My leg had fallen asleep, so I got up to go to the loo and make a drink. Surely it wasn't too early to have a cheeky wine as warm-up for tonight. I agreed with myself it was perfectly acceptable, and cracked open the rosé. Danny had messaged me again when I got back. I'd almost finished with the applications.

Danny - *So what are you up to? x*

Me - *Applying for jobs! x*

I pressed the camera icon and sent a picture of the organised chaos strewn in front of me.

Danny - *Wow! Busy girl x*

Me - *I know. I would be finished by now if you didn't keep distracting me! Lol. Wubu2?*

Danny - *Charming. What's that mean??*

Me - *What you been up to? ha ha x*

Danny - *Oooh! Not much to be honest. As I said, mostly working. Did go sunning it up in Turkey a few weeks back x*

Me - *Alright for some! Who did you go there with? Xx*

As soon as I'd sent it, I regretted it. I knew the answer would leave a sour taste in my mouth.

Danny - *Erica x*

Oh, how did I know it would be her?

Me - *I bet that was fun x*

I wrote without even thinking. Luckily, Danny didn't seem to read it in the sarcastic manner I had meant it.

Danny - *Yeah, it was good. We had a laugh most of the time*
x

Me - *Only most?*

Danny - *Lol, yeah. You've met Erica. Xxx*

I sure had. I didn't want to talk about her, so I put my phone down and finished the last ten envelopes I had left. By the time I'd finished that and the wine, I looked back to my phone and saw I had five new messages.

Danny - *Doing much tonight?*

- *??*

- *Are you there? x*

- *Where you gone? xxx*

- *Bye then, lol x*

Me - *Sorry! I was finishing up. All done. A busy day delivering tomoz x*

- *Just waiting on Kat to finish work. Off out tonight x*

Danny - *Brighton? xx*

Me - *No lol, Ebourne x*

Danny - *:-(x*

Me - *Sorry xx*

Danny - *Come to Brighton!! It'll be fun. Free drink on arrival :-)*

Me - *Drink! Is that it? Make it plural and I may think about it.*

Danny - *Drinkssssss then. Come on, not seen you in an age*
x

- *Don't you miss this face??? Xxxxx*

An image of him making puppy dog eyes and an over-exaggerated sad face popped up on my screen. I laughed out loud. I did miss him. I also knew there was no way Kat would agree to Brighton. Ben had a darts night planned with the guys, and said he would come and meet us later. She knew he wouldn't bother to go all the way to Brighton.

Me - *Hmmm, oh yes, I cry myself to sleep at night because I miss you so much, lol. Will ask Kat but you know she'll say no xx*

Danny - *Make sure you send her the picture! Xxx*

Me - *ha ha x*

Straight away, I reopened Kat's chat. Now the idea was in my head, I really wanted to go and see Danny.

Me - *Hey, hun, don't fancy Brighton tonight, do you? x*

I wondered if I would have even considered it if I hadn't had a glass of wine. She replied pretty much straight away. I was slightly miffed her boss had obviously left and she hadn't messaged me already.

Kat - *Oh. I thought we'd decided Eastbourne*

No kiss. Already hostile. This was a no-go, but I had to at least try.

Me - *I know, but we've been offered free drinks! x*

Kat - *From who? x*

Me - *Danny. At his bar. He misses us xx*

A double kiss to emphasise. Kisses in an IM were very important.

Kat - *Oh*

That was a pissed-off oh. I had read it many times before. Kat didn't do well with plans changing, especially when it jeopardised the other arrangements she had made with herself.

Kat - *When did you see Danny? x*

Me - *I didn't. He msgd me x*

Small white lie.

Me - *He didn't even know about me and Max x*

Subject change. Good move.

Kat - *Shut the front door! How did he not know? x*

Danny messaged.

Danny - *What did she say?*

I continued with Kat.

Me - *I know! That's what I said. Crazy.*

 - He wants an answer

Kat - *erm… well, I've already arranged with Ben about meeting*

Surprise surprise.

Kat - *And one of Ted's friends is DJing in V-bar tonight. I really wanted to see him.*

I sighed. I didn't know why I was bothered. I hadn't even spoken to Danny for months.

Me - *ok. I will tell him no then x*

Kat - *tell him another time xx*
Two kisses. She was feeling guilty.
Me - *ok cool x*
I clicked back on Danny's chat.
Me - *Sorry, no go x*
Danny - *Oh, man. No way fair! I was looking forward to seeing you xx*

My stomach flipped. He actually wanted to see me. 'Oh my God, Casey,' I spoke to myself. 'Calm down. He just means as friends.'

Me - *Me too! Offer still open for another night? x*
Danny - *Only if you promise it will be soon xx*
Me - *Promise xxx*

Chapter Sixteen

The music was on loud, the drinks were flowing, and Kat and I were in full party mode. Dresses, tops, and skirts were strewn across my living room. Eyeshadow, mascara, and make-up brushes collected on the coffee table. My full-length mirror from the bedroom was propped up against the back of my sofa, with a huge pile of cast-aside heels sitting in front, to prevent it from slipping.

After trying on at least ten different outfits, I had settled on my trusty little black dress. Kat was acting weird. She kept going on about looking our best tonight, but I figured it was because we were meeting up with Ben.

Two bottles of wine later, the taxi picked us up and took us to the hustle and bustle that was town. Walking into V-bar, I felt like an elderly woman walking into a playpark. The average age of the place was eighteen – and a young eighteen at that. The lower level was crammed with groups of girls and guys vying to get the bartenders', and each other's, attention. Standing at the back surveying the scene in front of me, I looked around and caught some infant looking me up and down.

'Hey,' he said, slow-nodding his head as he spoke. I half expected him to finish it with Joey's famous phrase from *Friends*. Then it dawned on me, this person was probably too young to know what *Friends* was. Not to be rude, I said hi back and turned my head away, looking out for the rest of the girls we were meeting.

'So,' he carried on, 'you want my number?'

I looked back, frowning, 'Erm, no thanks.' I looked away again.

'Oh, well then, can I have yours?'

I was grateful that Kat heard her name being called from the stairs and grabbed my hand and pulled me away.

'Oh God! Did you hear that guy?'

Kat laughed. 'You owe me one for saving you.'

Upstairs was even smaller than downstairs. With the DJ decks set up and our two tables. there was only place for a couple of others. As I took my seat. I saw Kat point in her ever-so-obvious way, as if to say, 'this is her'. Oh crap. I was being set up with the DJ. I glared at Kat, eyes wide, as she shrugged saying 'what?' all innocently.

She was saved by the bell, as Tracey turned up with a tray of shots. 'Sassy bitches all round, ladies.'

'Mmm.' I grabbed one. 'My fave.'

I loved the one-pound shots at V-bar. We clinked the plastic shot glasses, licked the whipped cream off the top, and downed the fruity strawberry liquor. As I set my glass down, DJ guy raised his eyebrows at me. I went from being mildly annoyed at being set-up, to downright insulted. It got worse later, when I found myself conveniently left on my own during his break. Kat was very insistent I had to stay to look after the drinks, and he came over to talk to me.

'Hi gorgeous, do you come here often? Ha, I'm only joking. How totally cringe, eh? Chat-up lines are the worst. Well, this is rather awks. Don't you just hate being set-up?'

No, I thought in my head. What I hate is being set-up with fat, balding, middle-aged DJs who actually use the word awks in a sentence. But instead, I smiled and just said, 'Yeah.'

'Well, I must say it's nice to meet you. Ted said you were a cracker and I gotta say, he was deffo right.'

Ted, a work friend of Ben's, had met me once at Kat and Ben's engagement party. Ted had no right to describe me as a Christmas table ornament. Out of politeness, I tried to make conversation with the guy.

'So, have you known Kat long?'

'No, actually until tonight I'd never met her.'

Great. So, she actually hadn't even met the guy she had agreed to set me up with. 'Oh,' was all I could say. I was giving up free drinks in Brighton for this.

'The name's DJ Dexx.' He held out his hand to shake mine, his 'FREE HUGS' T-shirt becoming glaringly obvious.

'DJ Dexx?' Really? Was he actually using his DJ name to introduce himself to a potential date?

'Dexter when I'm at home.'

'Oh right.' I gestured to myself. 'Casey.'

'I know. Does Casey wear lacey?' He belly-laughed. 'Maybe I will get to find out later?' He winked.

I sent Kat a text under the table. *GET BACK HERE NOW!!!*

'So, Casey, what do you do?'

I swallowed an extra-large mouthful of my drink and bluntly replied, 'Nothing. I'm between jobs at the moment.'

'Oh, cool. Well, I do a boring 9-5 job as an accountant, but on the weekends I like to spin the decks, the decks of steel.'

I couldn't take this any more.

'Sorry, Dexter, er, DJ Dexx, little girls' room calls. You don't mind watching the drinks, do you?'

'Oh, not at all, glad to be of service.'

I grabbed my bag and walked out the door, bolting downstairs to the exit instead of upstairs to the Ladies. Kat was standing in the corner smoking and talking to a group of guys out on a stag night. She caught my eye as I stormed over, and she knew instantly she was in trouble. 'It was Ben's idea.' She hid behind Stacey.

'I'm going.'

'He can't be that bad!',

'Spinning the decks of steel,' I quoted.

'Oh God. Let's go.'

After a few more bars and blagging free entry to Cameo nightclub, we joined the queue at the kebab shop. I needed greasy food. Talking to every person I saw as if they were long-lost friends, the wait flew by. 'Add me on Facebook,' I called out to a gaggle of girls as they left with their cheesy chips.

'Donna kebab wrap with salad and garlic mayo, please.' In other words, my usual.

'Make that two,' called Kat.

'Good choice.' I grinned. 'I think I'm a little bit drunkard,' I said, as we took our seats up the stairs to wait.

'That makes three of you.' We laughed. 'No, seriously, Case, I can see three of you.'

Our food arrived, and we tucked in like savage animals.

'A kebab just isn't a kebab unless you get grease dripping down your chin,' Kat said with a mouthful.

I swallowed mine and scoffed, 'Better than something else dripping down your chin.'

'Urgh! You're always lowering the tone.' She threw a napkin at me.

'You love it,' I joked. My internet data had run out on my phone, so I couldn't upload all the pictures I'd taken. I didn't know half of the people in them.

'How many people did we meet tonight?' I asked.

'I don't know. Do you remember that group of Polish guys?'

'Sadly, yes I do.'

We finished our food and started heading towards the nearest taxi rank.

'Kat, I thought we were meeting Ben.'

'Who?'

'Erm, your fiancé.'

Kat stopped in her tracks. 'Shit!' Her hands flew up to the top of her head. 'I promised him I would meet him in TJ's.'

'What time?'

'One.'

I looked at my phone; it was nearly three.

'Hasn't he rung you?'

She pulled a face. 'My battery died. He's going to kill me. He didn't even want to come to town tonight.'

'Gutted.' I couldn't help laughing.

'He's gonna go mad. He told me to make sure my battery was fully charged.'

'So you didn't?'

She shook her head.

I gave her my phone to ring him. She was right, he was furious. We met him around the corner at the taxi rank, where he ushered us straight into a cab. He didn't say a word the whole way to mine, Kat and I sitting in the back like naughty schoolgirls. The driver pulled up outside my flat, and I whispered to Kat 'good luck' before getting out the car. Just before I slammed the door, I said 'Bye, Benjamin' in a singsong voice. He hated his full name.

Once in the flat, I kicked off my heels and got a glass of water from the kitchen. Turning around to turn on the TV, I caught a glimpse of myself in the mirror. It gave me a fright. My signature red lipstick was smeared down my face, and my smokey eyes looked like black holes. As the home wi-fi kicked in, my phone erupted with sounds. Facebook notifications; friend requests; Messenger, WhatsApp; Snapchat.

I found an easy-to-watch American sitcom on the TV, then started working through the icons on the top of my phone screen. Kat had tagged me in a picture. I looked hideous. Mum had uploaded her holiday snaps and tagged me in them just to gloat. I had a few messages from Ben, asking where we were; the last one in capitals: *TELL KAT TO RING ME NOW!*

A message from DJ Dexx (also his Facebook name), saying sorry he'd seemed to have missed me.

7 friend requests; his was at the top and the first to be rejected. There was one more message, this one from Danny.

Danny - *Hope you guys had a great night. Looking forward to seeing you soon xxx*

I flopped onto the couch with my phone in my hand, and was out like a light.

Chapter Seventeen

I woke up with drool down my face, sticking me to the sofa cushion. Yuck. As I tried to roll over, my arse cheeks stuck to the leather where my dress had ridden up in the night. Urgh. I glanced at the clock. Seven-thirty. No, no, no. Why was it that in all the time I worked, I had needed three alarms to even get me up, but now I have nothing to do or nowhere to go, I am up before eight most mornings – even after a big night out. My mouth was dry, so I reached for my glass of water. The TV was still on. Some random programme highlighting what films were coming out in the upcoming months. Oooh, a new Johnny Depp one. I must tell Kat.

Kat! I remembered her and Ben. Oh no. My winding him up by calling him Benjamin as I got out of the taxi must have made the situation so much worse. I wondered if she'd text me. My phone! Where was my phone?

I looked under the cushions, searched down the back of the sofa. Did I even bring it home? Had I left it in the taxi? No, I'd seen the picture Kat tagged me in. I looked over to where my laptop lived, all neatly tucked away. I definitely wouldn't have put it away properly if I had used it last night, so I must have used my phone.

I looked to the floor. There it was, screen-down, luckily on a discarded handbag I had thrown there whilst getting ready. I picked it up; the screen was perfect, but the battery was dead. Forcing myself up and into the kitchen, I simultaneously plugged in my phone and flicked the switch on the kettle. There, on the breakfast bar, was the pile of envelopes ready for delivering today. Could they wait? I decided to think about it later.

My phone started to turn on as I concentrated on making

my cup of coffee. The familiar ping of a new Facebook message lured me away. It was Max.

Max - *Hi Case, hope you're ok. Sorry to msg u so early but I'm changing the curtains in the bedroom. Just fancied a change. Wondered if you wanted them back as I know Nan made them for us and u chose them. Let me know, no rush. M xx*

Just fancied a change? Max! It was hard work getting him to change his underwear, let alone buy new curtains. This had Lisa written all over it. The message had been sent at 5am. I pondered the idea that they had been out until three then spent the next two hours arguing why he still had bits of me dotted about his house, our home.

I pressed the home button, taking the message out of my view. I was feeling annoyed. Did he think I was stupid? He must have known I would have figured this out. I moved back to my cup, and held it in my hands. I started drumming my nails on the side. I was feeling really agitated. Why had this annoyed me so much? I thought back to the day that Nan and I had gone to buy the curtains. He'd had brown velvet hanging when I first moved in. Vile. Disgusting. Brown. Velvet. They had to go. Nan asked if she could treat us as a housewarming gift.

One of my secret favourite places to go is the Old Loom Mill on the outskirts of Hailsham. We used to bike or walk there from Polegate in the summer when I was a child. Even at that age, I would spend ages looking at all the different fabrics. We would get an ice-cream or a cold drink before heading back.

Pulling up in the car, I had smiled at the sight of the place. It seemed so much smaller now. It was so quaint and tranquil. Nan got all excited. She'd been looking for a new project. I'd done all the measurements she'd asked for, and even brought one of the brown curtains with me just in case I'd got them wrong. I had! I chose a beautiful poppy print with a plain red for a band at the top.

Nan found all the stuff she needed for lining, and rings for the top. She was like a child in a sweet shop. 'These are going to look beautiful,' she said.

We finished off our trip with a cream tea in the sunshine and a small walk along the cuckoo trail, before heading back. She made the curtains within a week, and got her friend to drive her to mine to deliver them personally. They were the nicest curtains ever. Max had loved them, and couldn't believe Nan was so talented. She'd given up her sewing box long before I met him.

Now, I looked over at my plain grey curtains thoughtfully. Why did I ever leave them there?

I went back to my phone and searched for Messenger. Once it was opened, my list of chats sprung up. Danny. I smiled as I remembered that he had messaged last night. I liked the fact that for some reason, at that time, he had been thinking of me. Putting that out of my mind, I clicked on Max's name and quickly typed a rant as a reply.

Max, as I appreciate your new girlfriend may not like the fact that I chose the curtains for the bedroom. I wonder if she actually knows I also chose the décor for most of the fucking house, and helped you to choose 80% of your wardrobe! You don't have to pretend it is your fucking idea. Yes, I would very much like MY curtains back that MY Nan put her hard work into. FYI I'm fine and don't particularly appreciate you msging so fucking early in the fucking morning!!!!!!!

I took a breath, held down my delete button until the message completely disappeared, then started again.

Hi Max, Thanks so much for thinking of me. I would love them back. I'm fine, thanks, and don't worry, I was up anyway.

As I pressed send, I said out loud, 'You fucking douche bag!' As immature as it was, it made me feel better for wimping out of sending the first message. I locked my phone and placed it screen-down on the side. I was staring at it still. I started worrying. Maybe I shouldn't get the curtains back. How was I meant to get them? Would I have to see Max? I had a vision of me walking up to his front door and *her* answering. Just the thought of it made me ill.

Why hadn't I put up more of a fight for him? We had been so good together. I subconsciously held my hand over my scar.

A flashback to the day in the hospital when the nurse boldly announced, 'I'm sorry, Miss Turner, but your baby has died.' He was so supportive, so kind, but also so angry at that nurse. Not for what she'd told us, just the way in which she had. Right there, in the waiting room, in front of all those women. All those pregnant women. He had tried to put in a complaint, but I wouldn't let him. I just wanted to put it behind me.

The woman. There had been a woman in the waiting room with me. She kept rubbing her bump. Her husband was holding their scan picture in his hand. Max was rubbing my knee continuously. Rubbing, rubbing. A continuous circular motion. He was nervous. I just couldn't stop staring at this woman. It had to be her twenty-week scan. Her hand linked through her husband's arm. She was wearing two rings, so I assumed they were married. She was smiling, happy. She looked up at me, probably sensed somebody watching. Her smile widened, and my face tried to mirror her expression.

'We just found out we are having a boy.'

Something had caught in my throat. I wanted a boy first. I would have been happy either way, but the idea of my daughters having a big brother appealed to me. To be honest, all we ever wanted was a healthy baby. A baby. I had been so nervous waiting for my results. To find out if I even had one of those any more.

'Congratulations,' I managed to force out, my voice small and weak. That's when the nurse appeared and told me my outcome. Told me that all hope was gone.

I don't know who had been more embarrassed. The woman had taken the scan picture straight off her husband and put it inside the plastic folder that housed her pregnancy notes. Her face had a slight tinge of red. Looking back up at me, we stared at each other for a moment, a tear slipping down my cheek. She mouthed 'sorry' at me, and I shrugged. This wasn't new to us.

I saw that same woman the other day in town. There she was, pushing a pushchair with a boy of about two or three sitting wide-eyed, taking in all the sights in front of him. She smiled at me as she passed, but I don't think she recognised me. I would never forget her face.

Ping. My phone went off.

Danny - *Hey, beautiful*

The words made me smile. It had been a while since anybody had called me that.

Me - *Hey, ugly!*

Danny - *Oi! Cheeky. Ugly?? With these dashing good looks?!?!*

A huge gawking selfie appeared on the screen, making me cringe. I knew it was meant to be a horrible picture, but this one looked shocking! A bit like one of those caricatures they paint in holiday resorts.

Me - *Aaaaargh! My eyes, my eyes. lol x*

Danny - *Lol x*
 - *So what you up to? x*

Me - *You don't wanna know! It involves curtains x*

Danny - *Sounds fun x*

Me - *It's not. lol*
 - *So what are you up to?*

Danny - *Thinking*

Me - *Oooh, does it hurt?*
 - *About what?*

Danny - *You honestly want to know?*

Me - *Hmmm, you've intrigued me now. Go on.*

There was a few minutes' pause whilst I stared eagerly at the screen.

Danny - *You*

I threw my phone down on the sofa next to me. It was as if the message had given me an electric shock. Why would he say that? We were friends. Yeah, I had had an attraction to him, a pull, but that was it. I mean, he had a girlfriend. Ok, I hated her, but he was still wrong to say that. Really wrong. I'm ashamed to admit, though, that once the initial shock had gone I quite liked it. The thought of a man, that man, thinking about me. I was being silly. My phone pinged.

Danny - *Sorry*

Me - *For what?*

Danny - *You didn't reply. Guessing I spoke out of turn.*

Me - *A little. What would your girlfriend say?*

Danny - *I know it's wrong, but since I found out you were single I can't stop thinking about you*

Me - *Really?*

Danny - *Really*

Me - *Oh x*

I didn't know what to say. Should I admit, 'I keep thinking about you, too. I used to think about you when I was lying in bed with your best friend.' Maybe there had been signs. One night, Danny took Max and I out to a brewery event. Free drinks were flowing, and I got very drunk very quickly. We all did. Max got so drunk he started to feel unwell and called himself a taxi. Danny grabbed him as he was sneaking away,

'Aw, mate, wimping out on me! What am I meant to do now? We're supposed to be going clubbing.'

'Sorry, mate.' Max struggled getting into the cab. 'Take Case. No point us all missing out.'

'No, babe,' I laughed, 'someone has to make sure you get in the house.'

'I'm a big boy. Go on, give Danny a night to remember.'

The devilish side of me imagined he had actually meant something sordid by that. Obviously, even in my drunken state, I knew he just meant a good dance, shots, and a dirty kebab. This wasn't the first time Max had headed off early. This time, however, was different.

Having not eaten a lot during the day, I had easily slipped past my comfortable level of alcohol consumption. I still knew what I was doing, but the lines between right and wrong were very blurry. Danny paid for us to get in, then grabbed my hand and ran me over to the three-deep crowded bar, putting me in front of him, his hands on my hips, pushing me through to the front. He had judged correctly that the all-male bar staff would choose cleavage over a slightly awkward-looking bloke. As soon as I'd gotten their attention, Danny started ordering drinks. A lot of drinks. Fish bowls, jelly shots, and Jaegerbombs. This was getting messy.

'It's a shame Max went home,' Danny shouted above the music, getting close to my ear,

'Oh, charming, am I not good enough company?'

'Oh, you're the very best. I'm secretly pleased he's gone,' he joked.

'Oh shush you, you'll make me blush.' I took a long sip of our shared fishbowl. My head started spinning. The music changed.

'Ooooh!' I squealed. 'I love this song. Dance with me.'

We rushed to the dancefloor. Danny was a great mover; I already knew this. Max wasn't a dancer. He would nod his head and tap his foot, but never in time. He loved music but had no rhythm. As much as I pleaded and begged him to dance with me, he always palmed me off to Danny.

Danny's eyes were struggling to focus as we moved around the crowded space. I had never seen him this drunk before. Still, he had the moves, swaying his hips and twirling me under his arm. There were a few stumbles from both of us, then at one point I fell off my heels into his arms. I was laughing and trying to stand back up until I looked up at his face and caught him staring at me. I knew that look. A look of longing, or was I seeing what I wanted to see?

Time froze, and the music and people faded away. I found myself staring back at him. He started to lean down further, his lips towards mine; he was going to kiss me. I was going to let him. His eyes closed as we got closer. Time moved slowly. I closed my eyes and got ready for what was about to happen. I tilted my head further upwards and, just as I started to feel his breath on my face, I flung my hand up and placed my fingers against his lips, gently pushing him away. His eyes flew open and he looked horrified.

'I have to go.' I reached up to speak into his ear, suddenly feeling very sober.

'Huh.'

'I need to go home to Max.'

Danny looked confused for a minute. 'Yes. Max.'

I decided he looked confused because he was wondering where the girl he thought he was about to kiss had gone. I ran out of the club, jumped into the nearest cab, and we never talked about that night ever again.

The dangers of alcohol. I doubt Danny even remembered. The next time I was out dancing with him, I may have noticed him look away when I caught his eye, but I assumed – or hoped – I was being paranoid.

Now, all these years later, I'm staring at the screen, seeing him telling me he has been thinking about me. And now I can't help but wonder, has he always felt this way?

Danny - *Is that all you have to say? Oh?*

Me - *What else can I say?*

Danny - *I don't know. Something.*

I waited a while, thinking. What is right and what is wrong? It is wrong to encourage, but then it isn't right to lie. I pondered for a while before typing.

Me - *I've been thinking about you, too.*

Chapter Eighteen

The day I had been dreading for weeks finally came. It was Kat's cousin's baby shower.

'You will come, won't you, Casey?' Laura had willed me at Kat's mum's fiftieth a month before. 'I would love you to be there.'

I smiled back to her as best I could. 'Sure, Laura, I wouldn't miss it.'

A concerned Kat watched me over Laura's shoulder as she lunged forward to hug me, all excited, before rushing off to the toilet, announcing to the room this must be her hundredth time today. 'I swear this baby has taken up camp on my bladder!'

Kat stepped into the empty space she'd left. 'You know, you really don't need to go. Laura will totally understand.'

'It's fine.' I shrugged. 'It's nice of her to ask me.'

'It will be hard.' She squeezed my arm.

I nodded. 'Life has to go on, Kat. Unless you think me suddenly coming down with a highly allergic reaction to pregnant women would be believable.'

My 'everything is ok' mask was growing more bearable to wear, but it didn't stop it being heavy and uncomfortable. The longer I wore it, the prouder I was of it. It had gone from being a comfort blanket, to war paint, and now full-blown armour.

At the time of the invite, the baby shower had seemed miles off. I felt I had a lifetime to prepare, but now it was here it brought back all those painful memories. The house looked like a tissue paper factory had exploded. A mash of pinks and blues turned into giant bottles and nappies. It was swarming with kids. Newborns swaddled in blankets, toddlers feeling their way around the furniture, and bored pre-teens chasing their siblings to the shout of 'slow down' from their parents.

Kat and I were the only childless singletons in the room, but at least she had a ring on her finger.

'So, Casey, why aren't you married?' one of Laura's friends asked, whilst whipping out a breast and attaching little Charlie.

My thumb felt along the empty space on my ring finger where my promise ring used to sit. I used to play with it when I got nervous or found myself in uncomfortable situations. Even now, two years later, I still sometimes felt it there.

'I don't know, really.' I shrugged. 'Maybe I just scare them away.'

'You were with that dishy Max for years,' Laura chimed in. 'What happened?'

'We just grew apart.' I didn't think talking about failed pregnancies was the best plan at a baby shower.

'Oh, such a shame. Pretty little thing like you should have been snapped up by now.'

'I quite like being single,' I lied.

'Oh nonsense,' quipped Tabatha, super-mum to Tobias and Ethan 'Yes, I'm sure it's nice to have your own space, of course, but it must get lonely.'

I laughed it off. 'I have people to talk to.' I tapped my phone. 'Good old technology.'

'Oh, but it's not the same.' That was Helen, the first one. 'A phone cannot replace human contact. I don't know what I would do without a cuddle from my Tony at night.'

'We've set a date!' Kat suddenly shouted, obviously throwing herself under the bus to save me.

'Ooooh goody. When?' Laura gushed. She loved weddings. She'd told me this at every family get-together of Kat's I'd ever been to.

'15th March.'

'How long's it been?' gaffed Tabatha. 'Ten years?'

'No, seven. To the day. We are getting married on the anniversary of the day he asked me.'

'Oh, that is the sweetest!' Laura's hormones had her close to tears.

'Quick, Casey, that gives you just under six months to bag

a man, then you and Kat can be pregnancy buddies.' The trio were very pleased with this plan, clapping and cooing. and calling, 'Yes, hurry up, Casey.'

'Leave it, guys.' Kat looked uncomfortable.

'What! It's a great idea,' laughed Tabatha, 'unless you are one of *those* women.' As she emphasised the word 'those', she gave Helen a look. I felt everyone was staring at me. I tried to speak but I couldn't. My hands felt clammy. I dug my nails into my hand.

'You are, aren't you?' Helen accused.

'Guys, please.' Kat tried to help.

'You're one of those women that doesn't want children, aren't you?'

I started feeling like a caged animal, backed into a corner.

'No,' I managed to cut in, creating them to finally fall silent. 'I'm one of those women that can't.' And with that, I flew out the door.

I'd only gone about three steps out of the front door before I realised not only had I left my handbag inside that held my purse and mobile phone, but I had also left my jacket that had a small pocket which housed my emergency fiver. I considered turning round and going back in, but decided instead to head straight to the bus stop at the end of the road.

With nowhere else to go, I sat there, eyes closed, head tilted back against the bus timetable behind me. I heard a bus pull up and stop, the doors open. I knew the driver would be watching me, checking if I was about to suddenly jump up and get on, but I just stayed there, eyes closed, breathing deeply. I had considered getting on, sitting in a quiet corner of the bus, and travelling around and around for the rest of the day, but even if I wanted to I didn't have any money.

The doors closed, and the bus moved away. Every now and then, I heard footsteps walking past me. The tip-tap of boots on the pavement got louder then quieter, as they passed me by. One of the sets of footsteps didn't get quieter again. They stopped.

'I got us some cake.'

I slowly opened my eyes, letting them adjust to the bright

72

light of summer, and saw Kat standing in front of me with two perfectly wrapped pink parcels.

'Have I ruined the party?'

Kat perched next to me, plonking cake in my hand.

'Helen and Tabatha's faces were a picture! Laura cried, and then Ethan took his nappy off and smeared shit all up the stairs.' By now, she was laughing hysterically. 'So, I think you have been fully forgotten about.'

'Oh my God.' I couldn't help laughing along. 'What did your auntie say?'

'She's been after Uncle Martin to change the carpets for years. It will give her a perfect excuse.'

'He will just get them cleaned, surely?' I licked some butter icing off my finger.

'Can't you hear her?' Kat did her best impression of her posh aunt Cath. 'Oh Marty, I know they did such a good job of the cleaning, but all I see when I look at my lovely cream carpet is faeces.'

We finished our cake, and I took my bag off Kat. As I took the handle, we both felt the bag buzz.

'Oh yeah, sorry, I forgot to say it's doing that. You probably have a message or something.' I quickly dived into my bag. 'Look at the urgency,' Kat continued. 'Are you hoping it's your mystery man?'

'I've told you there is no mystery man. He's just a friend.'

'A friend that messages you fifty times a day, and you're keeping them secret from your bestie?' She pretended to look hurt.

'I'm sorry, but I have already told you it's complicated.'

'Hmmm. That means one of three things. He's old, he's ugly, or he's married.'

With mock offence, I assured her he didn't fit into any of those categories.

'Ah,' she said, as if I had just given her a clue, 'he is a he, though. I was starting to think you were becoming a fanny licker!'

'Well, babe, if I did, you would be the first to know.' I stuck my tongue out at her and wiggled it jokingly.

'Good to know. Now,' she jumped up, 'let's go somewhere else and get shit-faced.'

'Finally. I thought you'd never ask.'

I hadn't told Kat I'd been talking to Danny, because I knew she wouldn't agree with it. She hated cheaters as much as I did, especially after what she went through with Sean. In my defence, we weren't cheating. We were only talking. Deep down, I knew it was wrong. I would have been foolish if I had thought otherwise, but all I kept telling myself was: I am single. If he was choosing to message me, that wasn't my fault, was it?

Nothing had happened, as such. Yes, we had talked about sex. No, we hadn't talked about sex with each other. Well, not directly. Not at first. We may have started a few what-if scenarios. What-if he was single? What-if he happened to turn up on my doorstep? Obviously, when he first suggested he could turn up one night, horny and wanting me but was still with Erica, I said a blunt no. No, I would not let him cheat on his girlfriend with me. In fact, it wasn't just him. Johnny Depp could turn up asking to whisk me away for a dirty weekend, and I would have to turn him down because I knew he was in a relationship. Never under any circumstance would I be the other woman. I was worth much more than that.

As time went on, and our conversations got longer and closer together, I slightly changed my story. I told him that as much as I truly believed that I would say no, there was always that slight chance I wouldn't be able to help myself. I said I still didn't believe in cheating; that would never change. But there is no possible way to say never. Different situations have different outcomes. Like if I was drunk or tired, or drunk and tired, I would still like to say no but there was more of a chance that I could possibly change my mind.

Now, a whole six months after that first message, we had gone way beyond that. I had admitted to him that yes, without a doubt, one thousand percent, if he turned up on my doorstep and actually wanted to cheat on his girlfriend, I would let him. But I also didn't believe that he would be able to do that to her,

74

as much as he may want to. They had been together years, and even though he had plenty of opportunities to do so, running the bar, her working away for weeks at a time, he had actually stayed faithful this long.

He told me he had never even considered cheating before now. I wasn't stupid, I knew there was a chance he was just saying it to flatter me, but I didn't care because it was working. I was feeling amazing. The worthlessness I had felt after Max, had disappeared. We would stay up all hours talking about when we first met. The spark he felt, how he hated the fact he couldn't act on it because I was Max's girl. He told me things I'd never known. How he used to watch me tuck my hair behind my ear, and got jealous of the way I looked at Max. He told me he only went out and found himself a girlfriend, because he was so jealous seeing how happy we were that he wanted to try and get that for himself.

He made me feel so special from first message in the morning to last one at night, and I went from feeling guilty about Erica to resenting her for being the only thing in the way of me having him all to myself.

As much as I knew it was wrong, it made it exciting. I also knew the real reason I couldn't tell Kat. As much as she hated cheaters, she loved me so would no doubt tell me she understood.

But if I gave her my reasonings and showed her the messages, she would uncover Danny's sweet messages to be exactly what they were. They were proof that a guy would tell a woman anything to try and get her into bed. See, I couldn't tell Kat, because as long as this was just between Danny and me, I could pretend that what he was saying was real.

Chapter Nineteen

There's that song that goes 'money makes the world go around'. I don't believe that. I think sex does. Sex is everywhere. It doesn't help now, with technology the way it is, that sex is literally a click away. You have easy access to porn, dating sites aimed to getting a shag within the day, and escorts who – let's be honest – are, in most cases, just a nice name for a prostitute. Ok, that's possibly not completely true, but prostitution does still go on today. Problem is, people don't even need them any more.

So many girls these days use their bodies to get what they want. You can't go to a club without seeing gorgeous girls with flesh on show everywhere, flirting with a guy three times their age so he will buy them drinks. Beautiful models married to doddery old men with bank accounts more stuffed than their fake tits.

Maybe they are the perfect pair. Money and sex, sex and money. The world isn't changing, people's perception of it is. People just know more than they ever did. Once upon a time, it was easy to turn a blind eye. Whores hid in dark alleyways or in sectioned parts of the city. The seedy, secret side of civilised society. Now, all you have to do is flick to the back of the local free paper, or do a quick internet search, and there they are! The longest running profession.

They have TV shows on late at night talking about how to improve your sex life. Blow job techniques, how to give the best hand jobs. Other programmes dedicated to all things sex, presented by blokes with dodgy accents, surrounded by half naked, big breasted women. We learn about the artist that paints with naked people rolling on huge canvasses, and the porn stars that have bedded thousands of women. There are sex party cruises, where they spend a whole weekend naked on a ship, shagging every person that takes their fancy.

There are TV dramas based in brothels, or following the weekly antics of an escort. These men – and women, of course – pay for anything from straightforward missionary position to full-blown bondage. Did you know that some fully-grown men actually pay women to dress them and treat them as babies? They sleep in giant cots and wear nappies. I used to think these people were weird. Freaks. Perverts. These programmes showed the person behind the fetish. Hard-working businessmen with the weight of the world on their shoulders, knowing that one little slip-up would be disastrous, and wanting a way to escape from the stresses of it all for just a few hours in their 'mummy's' arms, with a bot-bot and a blankie.

Being an adult is hard sometimes; I can't really blame them. I still don't fully get it, but who am I to judge? Sex is no longer taboo. *Sex and the City* had six series and two films, with thousands of followers; *Fifty Shades of Grey* had women and men of all ages cramming into the cinema, vanilla couples getting a peak into the sordid world of S and M. We read sex. We watch sex. We talk sex.

I love to talk about sex. It's never bothered me. No subject is off-limits. The problem is, I would answer a question about sex in exactly the same way I would answer a question about how I like my tea. Milk? Sugar? Missionary? Doggy? Sex fascinates me. So, when anybody asks me anything, I just answer the question.

What I didn't factor into the equation was that when Danny asked me what my favourite position was, or if I liked it when a guy went down on me, I answered in a matter of fact way. But he's a man. As a man, hearing a woman say that she loves loads of different positions and telling him why she loved them, he automatically imagined I was describing what I'd like to do with him. What to me was just an ordinary conversation about my favourite subject, was like a long line of dirty conversations to him. All I needed to do was add the odd 'oooh' and 'aahh'.

So, as we went on, his questions got dirtier and it was only then I started to realise what he was up to. The more he asked, the more detailed description I gave. I began to realise he was really enjoying it. I started to enjoy it, too. Knowing that I could turn Danny on without being anywhere near him, started turning me on, and our exchange of words escalated to an exchange of pictures and videos. Ok, I knew then I had really overstepped the line, but I started to crave him.

I'd watch my phone for a sign that he was online, or wake up late checking for my usual good morning greeting. I was hooked. Sometimes, though, we would be mid-chat, things were getting interesting… and suddenly he was gone. Deep down, I knew these were the times that Erica was home. She had probably walked in, thrown her bags down in the hallway, and demanded he carried her to bed and ravaged her. I preferred to believe he'd just lost internet or something.

I would think about how I would have felt if it was Max sitting up late at night talking to women. The idea that maybe he had. Our relationship had been really strong for years, but then maybe Erica felt the same way about hers. When things got bad and Max and I became distant, I would go to bed first. After my third miscarriage that resulted in my surgery, I hardly ever got out of bed. Maybe, just maybe, Max had found somebody to talk to during that time. And I wouldn't have blamed him. I wasn't the girl he had fallen in love with any more; well, not at the time.

We had been strangers sharing a house. We didn't even share a room for a long time. What if he had cheated on me in this way months, or even years, before we actually split up? He could have had this whole other life I knew nothing about. How would I feel if I was in Erica's shoes? So many times, I considered ignoring Danny's messages. So many times, I wanted to tell him I couldn't do this, but when it came down to it I couldn't give him up.

Erica had treated me as the enemy from day one, at least now I was giving her a reason to hate me. I have said before that I wasn't a bad person, but I think we all have a little bad in us. Danny brought that person out of me, and I liked it.

Kat and I had gone out for drinks with Katherine from her work. We were having a laugh, and the drinks were flowing.

'So, Casey, I don't think I've really seen you since just after you and Max split. How long's it been?'

I stirred my drink. 'Two years.'

'Two years! Blimey. Where the fuck has that time gone?'

'I know,' I laughed. 'Crazy.'

'Yep, fucking crazy.'

Katherine had four kids. and was one of the funniest women I had ever met. As much as she watched her words when her children were around. the second she put on her make-up and heels and got the hell out of her house, she swore every few words. I found it so funny; it was like she suddenly had freedom.

'So, who've you been seeing?' she questioned.

'Erm, well, nobody really.'

'What the fuck do you mean nobody? Kat, have you heard this shit?'

She was just coming back from the bar, and I started to feel myself blush. Sex I can talk about; my singleness I can't.

'Sorry, they are out of house, so I got you Smirnoff, and that guy there got us Jaegers. What were you guys talking about?'

'Casey has had no fucking guys since Max!'

'Shhh, keep your voice down. I don't need the whole pub to know,' I jumped in.

'Sure, she has,' Kat started. 'What about… Oh no, that was Kim… erm, I'm sure, maybe, but wait that means it's been… Oh my God!'

'Yep,' continued Katherine, 'two fucking years.'

'Sorry. Katherine. do you wanna speak up? There's a guy in the pub down the road didn't quite hear that,' I snapped. 'It's not that big a deal, it's only sex.'

'Only sex!' Kat laughed. 'Never thought I would hear you say that. I always put you down as one of those addicts. You love sex.'

'Kat! I love *Breaking Bad*, too, but you don't see me going out trying to make crystal meth, do you?' I was starting to

79

wish I hadn't come out.

Katherine had started looking round the bar. I asked her what she was doing.

'Trying to find you some bootay! Help get you back on that bicycle you were pushed off.'

'Oh God, no, I couldn't.'

Katherine's head snapped towards me. 'And why the hell not?'

'It's complicated.' I downed my Jaeger and made good progress on my vodka, whilst the girls both stared at me waiting for a proper answer. Gradually, I looked back up at them. I took a deep breath and then finally said, 'I'm nearly thirty.'

'So,' Katherine said, 'I'm thirty-five. Nothing wrong with that.'

'Yes, hun, but you've had the same husband since you were seventeen. He's seen your body almost every day for eighteen years.'

'So, what's your point?' Kat sucked on her straw.

'The point is, the last person that saw me naked was Max. He watched my body age and change for all those years, and it's changed for another five years since. I've put on weight, I have my scar and stretchmarks and, well, my boobs aren't awful but the last time I got naked with someone new for the first time, I was only nineteen. Everything pointed in the right direction.'

'Ahhh, poor little Casey.' Kat tilted her head to the side mockingly. 'Can't find love with her old, saggy, lady bits.'

I threw a beer mat at her

'You're thinking about it far too much,' said Katherine. 'You've made it into a thing. An issue. As you said, it's just sex. Rather than working yourself into a frenzy worrying about how long it's been, just do it. Embrace change. Rip off the bandage. Look around, pick a guy at random, close your eyes, and open your legs.'

'What, here?' Kat asked, as I gave Katherine an exasperated look.

A burst of noise came over from the other side of the bar.

A gaggle of girls clapping and wooing as a young woman was led to a single chair by a man in a police uniform.

'Oh my God!' squealed Katherine. 'Is that a stripper?'

I think it was obvious by the way he ripped open his shirt that he wasn't a real policeman. Watching half naked men get drizzled in baby oil is pretty much every woman's guilty pleasure, so we – along with a few of the other females in the room – wandered over to get a closer look.

'Oooh, choose him,' Kat said, biting her lip.

I laughed and nudged her to shut up. It was only then that I looked at the stripper's face and realised I actually knew him! Steve Easton had been in my year at school. The last time I had heard anything about him, he was studying mechanics at college.

I suddenly wasn't sure what to do. Should I look away? Why is it ok to watch a complete stranger strip down to his birthday suit, but when it's someone you know you feel like a bit of a pervert? He was quite good, though, as far as strippers go. Some have nothing to them; they just rip off their clothes, do a little wiggle, and run off with a shit-load of money for doing nothing.

Steve actually had a talent. If I pretended he wasn't stripping, I could watch his dance moves all day. He threw a tiny pair of shorts in our direction, and Katherine caught them and started jumping about with them in the air as if she had just won the World Cup. Her husband was her polar opposite. Quiet and reserved. Katherine was a bloody nutter. They loved each other, though; it was obvious when you saw them together.

Kat was clapping away, screaming 'Off, off, off!' I guessed she didn't remember Steve from school. If she had, she would probably have been screaming something a lot different at him.

Steve's toned torso used to look a lot different in his younger years. As he finished his act and kissed the birthday girl on the cheek, the other girls – including Katherine – ran over with their mobiles, trying to take selfies. Kat ordered me to get his card so I could book him for her hen night, and pushed me in his direction. His physique had definitely changed since school, but what about the rest of him? He wasn't really a person I had spent a lot of time with at school, and that was by choice.

He had been a horrible boy. Mean and nasty. He thought being horrible made him look cool. He had always been bad enough when the boys were there, but the things he used to do to look good in front of the girls had been simply idiotic. He loved making fun of my name and pulling my hair – not hard, but it used to drive me crazy. I remember once he thought it would be really funny to lift up my skirt and show the whole class my bare arse. What? Thongs were really in at the time. There was even a song about them.

I ran out of class and hid crying in the toilets for the rest of the lesson. He called me knicker-less for the rest of the school year, which soon caught on with all his flock of brainless morons. It would be an insult to the animal to call them sheep.

Towards the end of that year, he had decided to ask me out. Of course, I said no without hesitation. The next day, I said yes to Neil Camson. On the way to maths, Steve slammed Neil's arm in the door and broke it. Poor Neil. I felt so bad for him at the time. Not bad enough, apparently, as a week later I dumped him – with the help of my friend Lizzie – for Jackson Thomas. His cast lasted a hell of a lot longer than we did.

Now Steve posed and pouted for his fan club, then made his apologies and broke away to finish picking up the discarded items.

'I put you down as more of a streaker than a stripper.' The night of our leavers' prom flashed through my head, Steve and his cronies running through the ballroom of the Hydro hotel stark bollock naked. It was the first time I'd seen a real penis. Put me off, if I'm honest.

'Well, well, well, Casey Turner. Long time no see. A streaker?'

'Your stunt at the Hydro.'

Steve chuckled to himself. 'I was such a dick at school.'

'Oh, so you actually know? That's lucky. I thought I was going to have to break it to you.'

'Yeah.' Steve shuffled a little awkwardly. 'You didn't like me much, did you?' I shook my head. 'I was kind of a jerk, I know. I had a lot of shit going on back then and wasn't sure how to process it. My mum used to, well, look, there's no excuse.'

I felt a bit bad. I picked up the shirt that was by my feet and passed it to him.

'Why don't you let me go get dressed, then I can buy you a drink and prove to you I'm not the same guy you knew back then?'

I thought about it for a minute then nodded an agreement. I've always believed in second chances.

Chapter Twenty

Staring at my empty glass, I started to think he might have done a runner out the back door. Kat and Katherine got all excited when I told them what he had said. They hatched a plan to move onto the next bar and, if I had any doubts or didn't like him, I could leave and head straight to join them. I agreed, and as they left Katherine grabbed my hand and said, 'We'll be just next door, kid, but I sure to God hope I don't see you again tonight. Give him one from me.'

Finally, he emerged from the back room, swinging his gym bag over his shoulder. He had certainly been worth the wait. This man knew how to dress. From his Gucci shoes to his Armani shirt, this guy oozed style. I giggled slightly at the reverse order of this evening. First, I had seen him naked, then fully clothed. As nice as the first was, the latter was so much better.

Max had never cared too much about how he looked. Scruffy t-shirts and low-slung jeans. I never minded. I actually quite liked the way he dressed, and borrowing his tees to slob around the house in was a bonus. But there was something very sexy about a well-dressed man. It would be a shame to ruin it. What if this evening did end up getting naked and dirty? I wouldn't want to undress him. Like when you get a beautifully wrapped present at Christmas. You can't wait to see what's inside, but you want to keep the parcel intact. In this case, I had already seen what was inside.

'That's a very big bag for a very small costume,' I joked.

'I actually did come straight from the gym. This isn't my usual job, stripping. The birthday girl is a friend of my sister. I was doing her a favour. Be right back.' And he headed to the bar. 'Hey, Trina, pint for me and same again for the beautiful lady.'

How sweet, I thought, but also hoped the barwoman wouldn't have confused my earlier vodka and coke for Katherine's ouzo. He appeared back at the table, bragging that he'd managed to get free drinks for the week and a huge pile of ironing done, just for helping Izzy out.

'So, what is your actual job?'

'I keep people company.'

'What, like one of those personal helpers, for disabled people or the elderly?'

'Not exactly. I keep people company at parties and functions.'

'What, like a date?'

He leant back, stretched his legs out in front of him and had a smug look on his face whilst he kind of shrugged. I tilted my head slightly and focused on his face. He bit his lip and looked away.

'You're an escort!' I accused.

He laughed, but didn't agree or deny. 'What does it matter what I do?'

'You are, aren't you?'

'So what if I am. I'm good at it.' I couldn't disagree with that. We had only been sitting with him a few minutes and I could see he was charming. I could imagine he would be great at the small talk and chit chat. I could see he could give compliments, check. I could see he was handsome; check. He had to look good; check. Worked out; check.

Blimey, I had chosen to let my guard down and have drinks with a guy who was paid to fuck women.

'Let me put you straight on that,' he jumped to his own defence. 'I am not a gigolo. I am not paid for sex. What I do is completely legal and above board. Women pay for my time.'

I crossed my arms and leant back in my chair. 'So, you don't actually have sex with your clients?'

He stared me in the face for a while, completely straight-faced, before cracking a smile. 'Well, what I choose to do in that time is my business.'

We both burst out laughing, whilst I threw a bar mat at him

and called him a pig.

'So, how did you go from trainee mechanic to escort?' I was genuinely curious.

Turns out, Steve did really well with his mechanics course and had a full-time job lined up in his dad's friend's garage for when he left college. He did that for a few months, but the business wasn't doing too well. As last in, technically Steve should have been first out if it got to the point they needed to fire people, but he knew his boss would never fire his friend's son.

One night, he went out with the lads and saw some gorgeous, 'seriously hot' – in his words – woman, sitting at a table towards the back of the bar. He kept watching her sitting alone, and after a short time decided to try his luck. He started talking to her, giving her a few of his best chat-up lines. He thought she was interested.

She explained to him that she was on a date, but handed him a card with her number on and said he should give her a call as she had a business opportunity for him.

'Well, I go back to the guys, who rip it out of me that I got nowhere. But there was me with a number, so as far as I was concerned, I was on a winner. Anyway, this mega-old guy walks in and goes straight over to my woman. As he gets there, she jumps up, cradles his face in her hands, and plants one straight on his lips. I mean, he was like could-be-her-grandad old.

'I thought something was fishy. So, I got a bit pissed off, like angry, why give me her number when she's dating a grave-dodger? Maybe she was just trying to line someone new for when the old guy snuffed it. I decided to ring the number then and there and have a go at her while she was sitting with the bloke. To ask her if I should tell him she's handing her number out to anyone who asks.

'I dig out my mobile and type the number in. The whole time, she's all over this guy, and I wait for her to jump up and answer. She doesn't. Some woman answers the phone. *Lovely Ladies*, she says in this really seductive tone. I stutter for a minute, not really registering what is happening. I get more

86

angry. She's not even given me her number! Then I look at the card and see a name. So, I say, "Crystal gave me this card, about a business opportunity. I'm sorry, I think it was a wind up."

'The woman on the phone says, "Ahhh Crystal, she is one of my best girls. If she thinks you are good for the job, I trust her judgement." I was like: What job?'

'So, Crystal was an escort?' I queried.

'Well yeah, it was obvious once they'd told me. Explains the old guy. Basically, they were trying to sort out a male escort company to run alongside their ladies' one, and before I knew it I was first on their books. The rest is what they call history. I quit the garage and saved anybody having to be fired.'

'How long have you been doing it?'

'Eight years.'

'So, I'm guessing you aren't married?'

'Pfft. Nah. I'm not the marrying kind. Don't see the point. Every relationship I've ever had has ended, not to mention my mum and dad and everyone else around me. Why would you want to be tied to someone you don't even like any more?'

I found that really sad. Was it true? Did true love always have to lead to heartache? I had to agree that, so far, I hadn't had much luck, but it didn't stop me from wanting to keep trying. Ok, I may have been finding things hard at the moment, but it didn't mean I was giving up.

We drank, we talked, we drank some more, then I got the text to say my taxi was just about to pull up.

'Well, it was really nice to see you again. I've enjoyed tonight, just chatting about the old days and stuff,' he said.

'Yeah, it's been great,' I agreed. 'God, if someone had bet me money we would be sitting in a bar together one day, having a heart-to-heart, I would have lost!' I got up to leave and Steve hugged me, placing a kiss on my cheek as he did so.

'I hope we can do this again some day,' he said, as I walked away.

As I reached the door, Kat and Katherine's words rang in my ear. 'Steve?' I called back. 'We don't have to wait for another day. We could, erm, have a nightcap. Maybe?'

Without saying a word, Steve grabbed his bag, swung it over his shoulder, and followed me out of the pub and into my taxi.

I had realised that Katherine was right when she said I had made it into a thing. I could never just randomly shag somebody I didn't fancy or have any connection with, but one-night stands were not something I hadn't experienced before. Was I ashamed about that? Well, no. I never used to be. I wasn't proud of it either.

You may ask why that was, and the answer is simple. It didn't really matter all that much. When I was applying for jobs, there wasn't a section on the paperwork that asked how many sexual partners I'd had, or what the average length of my relationships had been. Steve was just going to be a number in a line of numbers. He was not the first guy I'd planned to fuck without feeling, and I very much doubted he would be the last.

Even talking to Danny had started making me terrified. I had to have every faith in his faithfulness, because I needed to know that I didn't have to worry he would suddenly turn up at my door one day asking me to get naked with him. And if he did, would it be his relationship with Erica that stopped me, or this hang-up I had? Steve was going to be my cure. My ripped-off plaster. My practice run. I just hoped I could prove to myself I was still up for the job.

When we got back to mine, my confidence was shot. We had kissed in the cab. I kissed him first; I kissed him to stop him talking. I had to stop him talking. Not because I didn't like what he was saying, not because his conversation was boring. I kissed him, because the more he talked the more I worried about what was about to happen.

Kissing him didn't stop me thinking, but it was a welcome distraction. It was so nice to feel someone's lips on mine again. We stopped for long enough to pay the cab driver – Steve left him a sizeable tip – then continued kissing going up the stairs. Tripping over each other, knocking against the handrail. I was in the motion. We were going to burst through the door straight into my room. That's how I planned it. That isn't what happened, though.

First of all, I couldn't find the key. It wasn't in my handbag or coat pockets; not the first five times I checked. But it happened to be in my bag the first time that he looked. As I finally swung the door open, I pushed Steve in ahead of me and pressed him up against the wall, going for a passionate kiss. I failed. Instead, I slammed his head against the wall.

'Shit. Shit, I'm sorry.'

He was laughing it off. 'It's ok, it's ok.'

'Shit, bollocks, shit. Oh fuck, I'm so sorry. I'm soooo sorry.'

The moment was over.

I decided I wanted another drink. I know I didn't need one, but I wanted one. Grabbing two glasses, four ice cubes, my emergency vodka bottle out of the freezer and rooting around in the fridge for some sort of mixer, I made us both a drink. They didn't make it to both of us, though. I stood in the kitchen and downed them both, before pouring two more and heading through to the living room and setting Steve's drink down in front of him.

'Hey, are you ok?'

'Ok? Yeah, course. Why wouldn't I be ok?' I necked my drink and slammed it back down. Steve had only taken a sip of his.

'You seem nervous.'

'Nervous? Me?' The most ridiculous nervous giggle escaped my lips. I picked up my glass and swiftly brought it up to my lips before remembering it was empty. Steve nudged his glass towards me.

'Relax.' He smiled and, as I picked up his glass, I breathed deeply and started to loosen up. I took a drink. A long, slow sip this time.

'Ok. Maybe I am a bit nervous. It's been a long time since I had a guy back here.' He knew all about Max; somehow, it had come up in conversation earlier.

'I'm not scary, you know. I don't bite. Well, not unless you want me to.' I must have looked horrified, because he continued, 'Hey, come on, what's wrong? It's only me.'

'We're gonna have sex.'

I had blurted that out without any warning. I didn't know I was going to say it, and Steve certainly didn't. He looked stunned. I stared at his face, waiting for it to change, but he didn't move. I started to doubt myself. 'That is why you're here, isn't it?'

He laughed, still in shock, I think. 'Well, yes. I did think maybe, perhaps, it may be on the table when you invited me here, but I never thought it was guaranteed. We don't have to —'

I jumped in, 'No, we do have to. I do. I mean, I want to. I really want to.' I downed the last of his drink. 'I'm ready.'

I launched at him for another passionate kiss, but my knee slipped off the sofa and our teeth clashed hard. Once the pain had gone, Steve looked me seriously in the face. 'What do you really want?'

I took a deep breath. 'Fuck me.'

Chapter Twenty-One

Having sex with someone new, for the first time after a long time, felt like dancing a dance you don't know the steps to. Like you sort-of know what you are doing, the moves which you know fit to the music you're listening to, but it all feels a little bit… weird. I found I kept apologising.

We would clash teeth or bump heads. I couldn't quite get my footing. I used to be good at sex; I could take control. Max had quite liked to take the lead, though, and I liked it so I let him. After almost ten years of doing things his way, I had forgotten my own. The lovely haze of vodka had disappeared somewhere between the living room and the bedroom, leaving me far too aware of my surroundings.

Steve had carried me through and thrown me on the bed. We ignored the clothes strewn around the room. If I'd known this was going to happen, I probably would have taken a few minutes to put them back into the wardrobe.

I couldn't help but compare the now to the then. How Max had gentle hands, and Steve was quite rough and grabby. How Max had soft lips, and Steve had a larger tongue. It intruded my mouth like an uninvited guest.

I had to remind myself he was actually invited. I wanted this. I needed this. I kept telling myself to stop thinking about Max, which only made me think of him more. When I closed my eyes, I pictured his face. But having them open felt strange, and then I couldn't help but notice things. Steve's chest was hairier. His stomach was flatter, more toned. His neck, his torso. Everything.

'Hey, baby, relax,' he said, kissing down my breast then my stomach. 'I want to taste you.'

I suddenly wanted to hurl. My mind wouldn't shut down

91

and I didn't really know what to do.

'Doggy-style!' I shouted out, jumping up and moving onto my front. Maybe if I couldn't see him, I would stop comparing.

It kind-of worked. I managed to get through the next thirty minutes without picturing Max. This was nothing like him. Steve was like a machine. I don't think I'd ever wished a guy to finish quicker in my life. When he finally did, and flopped over onto his side, I smiled awkwardly, said I needed the loo, and ran and locked myself in my bathroom.

Maybe he would leave. I really didn't want to walk out there and have a conversation. What if he asked for feedback? This was kind-of his job, after all. Any hints or tips for the future? He could have comment cards printed off for his clients. It hadn't been bad, not even a little bit. Just awkward and different, and if I had relaxed I'm pretty certain it could have been great.

I had just had sex with Steve Easton and I'd thought about my ex the whole time. I wished I had grabbed my phone before I'd come into the bathroom. I could have phoned Kat, and asked what I should do now. I realised if he wasn't quickly getting dressed and running out the door, he would probably start worrying how long I had been on the toilet. And as embarrassing as going out there would be, I thought that would be worse.

I was so happy to find I had left my dressing gown in there earlier that evening, because it saved me having to walk back in stark naked. As I entered the bedroom, Steve had just finished dressing, and he stood and turned towards me.

'Hey, are you ok?'

I gingerly moved in a few steps and leant on the doorframe, nodding. Some of my awkwardness subsided. He sat on the edge of my bed and started putting on his shoes. 'I'll get out of your hair.'

I walked further into the room, moving to my dressing table. 'I'm so sorry,' I said quietly, feeling embarrassed.

'Babe, you have absolutely nothing to be sorry about. It's my fault. You told me you felt weird about the whole situation.'

'Just so you know, I'm normally better than that.'

He laughed. 'Wow. I thought you were pretty good as it was, so hopefully some time I will get you on a good day.'

I looked down. 'Don't worry, babe,' he continued, 'I won't be expecting a call.' He pulled on his jacket. 'You know he's a fool, don't you?'

'Who?'

'Max. If you were mine, I would have never have let you go.' He walked over, kissed me on the head, and started to leave. 'I'll see myself out. You get some sleep.'

'Thank you. I'm exhausted. Do you need a cab?'

'No, I can walk from here.' He turned at the door. 'Oh, Case? Keep my number, just in case you change your mind.'

As I heard the front door close, I crawled onto my bed, hugged my pillow, and fell asleep on top of the covers.

Chapter Twenty-Two

Months passed. and the night with Steve became just a distant memory. I saw him a few times out and about. and we always shared a warm smile and greeted each other like old friends, with a friendly hug and a kiss on the cheek. I had become really grateful for him. Since that night, I'd managed to relax around men. I had started casually seeing a guy, and we had even managed to have good sex. Great sex, even. I had even started to stop thinking about Max.

My life was finally moving forward. I had a new job, a purpose to get up every day – well, five days a week. I, Casey Turner, now worked nine-til-five, just like my favourite Dolly Parton song. I felt like I was suddenly a grown-up. I didn't have anybody doing anything for me. As well as updating my sweatpants for work clothes, I had increased my friend circle.

Me and two girls at work had become good mates. We were like the three musketeers. Kat and Ben were coming out less and less, because it was so close to the wedding and money was tight. And as much as I loved being at theirs, I did sometimes feel like I was in the way.

On the other hand, Larissa and Christina were always game for a night out. Larissa's boyfriend sometimes joined us, and Christina's parents were always available to babysit. Everything was fresh and new, except for Danny. Danny had become the only constant. I still talked to him every morning through 'til night.

With Kat's wedding fast approaching, she had welcomed my new friends in the same way as I always had hers. They even received invites to the evening of the wedding. And so did Danny. Two weeks before the big day, Kat and I were busy writing out place cards when I saw Danny's name on the list.

'Oh yeah, my uncle's new wife is having a boob job the day before my wedding, so now she can't come. I figured as her meal was already paid for, it made sense to invite someone in her place, so I hope you don't mind that I asked Danny. I moved stuff around so he can be your makeshift date for the day, unless you want to ask Paul? I can uninvite Danny.'

Paul was the guy I had been seeing, but that had fizzled out. 'No, don't worry, it's cool. It would be rude to withdraw the invite now.'

Kat still didn't know about us. She knew we still talked, and sometimes commented how nice it was that we had stayed friends. I felt really guilty, because I had never kept anything from her before. Really, though, what could I have told her? How could I tell her about us when there wasn't even an *us*? Technically, we were just friends. The whole time I am seeing somebody, that is all we are. It's when I'm not that Danny ups the chat. I keep it clean, he likes to taint it. I could never sleep with one guy and sext with another. I'm not a cyber-whore.

Two days before the event, Danny text me saying he was gutted but he couldn't be my fake date for the evening.

Me - *Does Kat know?*

Danny - *Yeah sure, she understands*

Me - *What's so important?*

Danny - *Some work's come up. A friend needs my help.*

I was really disappointed. With Paul officially off the scene, I had been looking forward to the chance to spend the whole day and night with the man of my dreams without his girlfriend being in the way. Now, who knew what cousin or distant relative of Kat's I would be stuck with?

'It's a shame about Danny, isn't it?' I casually brought it up when we were getting ready for our night-before-the-wedding girly sleepover.

'Oh, he told you? I know it would have been lovely to have him as a guest for the day but, well, I think it's sweet of him.'

'Yeah, I suppose you're right.' I tried not to look disappointed. 'So, who's taking his seat?'

'Nobody,' she said, whipping off her top and putting on her pjs.

'Oh, but what about the meal? If you've already paid for it.'

'I said he could still eat it. The least I could do was still feed him.'

That wasn't like Kat. Chips off her wedding, but she lets him stop by and scoff his dinner? It didn't make any sense, but I knew better than to question her the night before her big day.

We settled down for an evening of hot chocolate, face masks, classic films, manicures, pedicures, and lots and lots of wine. As we settled down to bed, I checked my Facebook and saw that Kat had updated her status 34 minutes earlier.

Tomorrow, I'm going to be Mrs Ben Chapman!

Eeek, can't wait. Perfect last evening as Miss Clark with my sister-from-another-mister! I love you, Casey. Next, we will find your Mr Right xxxx

'I love you, too, Miss Clark,' I said aloud to her, whilst replying to a goodnight text from Danny. Maybe I already had.

Chapter Twenty-Three

Kat's wedding day was magical from the moment we opened our eyes. The sun was shining. A large bouquet of flowers was delivered from Ben, a bottle of champagne was dropped off from the groomsmen, and the other bridesmaids arrived just in time for the champagne breakfast Kat had wanted. Her mum surprised us with hairdressers and make-up artists, and her younger cousin Charlie was on hand with his camera to capture every moment of the day, as he was just getting into the last term of his photography course at college. Everybody was happy. Everybody was smiling. Especially Kat.

The cars arrived and we all dived in. Music blared, and we sang along to all of Kat's favourite tracks before pulling up to the church. The ceremony was long but beautiful. Kat's dad beamed with pride, her mum and aunties wiped away tears of joy. I even saw Ben shed a sneaky tear. The whole thing went without a hitch.

After the vows, we had photographs taken inside the church, then we had photographs outside the church. We detoured on the way to the hotel, and had photographs at Beachy Head with the beautiful scenery behind us. Once we arrived at the hotel, we entered the reception hall as our pre-packed cases were taken up to our rooms. I found my seat – Kat's handwritten place cards marking where we sat, with our menu choices written out in her and my best calligraphy. The tables looked beautiful. Huge cocktail glass centre pieces filled with lilac flowers, fairy lights, and diamantes.

I looked at the empty place next to me. Danny's name card was still there. I took it down and snuck it into my handbag. Suddenly a waiter appeared at my side. 'Courtesy of the bar,' he said, placing a drink down on a small square napkin.

'Erm, thanks.' I looked over at Katherine, who was sitting opposite me. 'They must have seen me coming!'

Katherine's husband Derek sat glumly by her side. He was a huge Seagulls fan and was absolutely gutted to be missing their home game. When anybody spoke to him, he pointed out that she had made him give away his tickets to her brother, who didn't really even follow football.

'I haven't made him do anything,' she defended herself. 'I just pointed out that I have full control over whether he gets any at all this year.'

Derek wasn't the kind of guy that would disappear on a night out, or fuck off for a weekend with his friends, and he was always happy to babysit so Katherine could go out... just as long as their Sky Sports subscription was up-to-date. Sport was his life. I always joked that if you cut him open, he didn't bleed blood but football facts, and results from the past forty years would spill out of him.

The barman appeared again with another drink. Katherine pointed to it. 'Who did you screw to get special privileges?'

I was so confused.

'Honestly, hun, I do not know.'

A loud commotion drew our attention to the other side of the room. Oh no! DJ Dexx. He seemed to have pushed his chair out as a poor waitress was carrying a tray of drinks past his table, sending the contents over one of Kat's aunties' heads. He jumped over and started furiously dabbing at her with a handful of napkins. Then he glanced up at me and provocatively raised his eyebrows.

'Oh God, that explains it.' I told Katherine about the night I'd met Dexter. I felt stupid for not even realising he would be here. I had been hoping I wouldn't have to see him ever again. Did he think that sending me drinks over would get him a date? I was considering whether I should go over and speak to him, but I was saved by my main meal.

Food eaten and speeches done, we raised our glasses to toast the happy couple. We had about an hour left before we moved into the adjoining party room, where the disco and bar were. Thinking about bars, I decided to wander through and get myself a drink, hoping that maybe if I kept my glass replenished, Dexter wouldn't send over any more. It would be good to stretch my legs anyway.

Weaving through the crowded tables, stopping to say hello and pose for photographs, I arrived and pushed open the heavy wooden door. I wasn't prepared and had not expected to see what was behind it. The giant bar, with sparkling lights and large display of optics and glasses, had three or four bar staff already busy serving; one was loading a full tray of dirty glasses into the dishwasher. Right in the centre, pouring out a tray of champagne, was Danny.

I stared at him, shocked and confused. He had said he wasn't coming. Why was he here? I must have looked really confused, because one of the bar staff who was on her way back into the dining room with a tray of drinks, asked me if I was ok.

'Yeah,' I muttered vaguely, still staring ahead. At this point, Danny looked up.

'Hey, Case, how do you like the uniform? Snazzy, huh?' He held both arms out like he was on the cross, champagne bottle still in hand.

Realising I wasn't quite ready to answer, he continued. 'Wow, look at you in that dress. Knew you were going to be stunning. Cor, you're going to make working tonight really hard, if you know what I mean?'

As he winked, I moved forward and practically hissed, 'What are you doing here? You said you weren't coming. You —'

He stopped me. 'Ahh, but did I?'

'What?'

'Say I wasn't coming? Technically, I told you I wasn't going to be your date today.'

He had me there. He hadn't actually said he wouldn't be here, but he had certainly implied it.

'You said you had to work.'

He pointed at the bottle of champagne and continued to pour. 'I *am* working.'

'You said you were helping out a friend.'

'Kat is my friend.'

He passed the full tray to a colleague who carried it through to the other room, and poured me a double vodka and coke.

'It was you! The drinks.'

'Ahh, did you think you had an admirer?'

'That guy is here, the one I told you about. Ben's friend, the DJ. I really thought it must be him trying to get a date or something. Imagine if I'd gone over to him; it would have been so embarrassing.'

The doors opened, and a few guests started to filter through, including Katherine. She had grabbed me a glass of champers on the way through.

'Bloody get those drinks pouring,' she said to Danny as she downed hers. 'He's doing my bloody head in. Won't stop moaning about the fucking football. Football, seriously! We've got a romantic setting, a lovely wedding, I've even booked a fucking room and have promised him the night of his dreams now he's finally had the snip, and all he cares about is the shitting, fucking football!'

Kat came flying in, her wedding dress streaming behind her. 'Oh my God, today has been a-maze-ing!' she sang. 'Danny, I can't thank you enough. He's amazing, isn't he, Casey? A- maze-ing.'

I had to agree with the bride. Who wouldn't?

We stood talking for a while, and I found it strange how normal things were. When I saw Danny in the flesh, we were always just Danny and Casey, Max's friend and ex-girlfriend. Nobody here knew that we had a secret connection. Nobody knew we had expressed feelings, and talked and shown each other what we liked. I found that exciting. Our little secret.

'Where's Erica tonight?' Kat asked Danny.

'Erm, she's in Milan.'

'Aww, it must be hard with her jetting round the world.' Kat turned to Katherine to explain. 'She's a model! I wish I was jetted round the world for photo shoots.'

There it was. That little reminder. She was always there. She should be. She was his girlfriend, after all. I was just…

100

well, I don't even know what I was. I suppose I was his secret; his dirty little secret. I knew he liked me, though.

When he spoke about her, he had no brightness in his eyes. He didn't even answer Kat about missing her. He just looked down and cleaned a glass. He didn't miss her. She had probably only flown out today anyway. I'm sure she had been there yesterday, because he hadn't messaged me much.

Lost in thought, I stood there whilst the others talked. Eventually, I snapped back to reality and looked over at Danny, who was staring at me. He smiled warmly, winked, and headed off to a side room with the empty champagne bottles.

It was time for the first dance. Ben and Kat swayed in a loving embrace with Etta James's words floating out of the speaker: *At last my love has come along*. I had a warm feeling inside me that I hadn't experienced in a very long time. I think I loved Danny. As soon as he realised he wasn't happy with her, we could get on with our lives. I was going to be happy. I deserved to be happy. We both did.

Chapter Twenty-Four

Waking up in my beautiful suite, I tried to remember what had happened last night. I knew we hadn't gone up to bed until very late. I smiled to myself as I stretched out, yawning. I had small flashes of the evening. Kat and I leading a group of ladies in the *Macarena*. Ben trying to lift Kat in the famous *Dirty Dancing* pose and nearly flinging her into the cake. Every memory I had was funny.

Somebody had been crying. Who was crying? I tried to clear my memory. Why did I drink so much? I was remembering something else. Danny. Yes, Danny had been there working. I kept talking to him. He was dancing. Yes, that's right. He finished work and came to join the party. We danced. What was it that woman said? The middle-aged woman sitting with Ben's mum. 'You two make a lovely couple.' Oh yes, that was it. I had been about to correct her, to tell her we were just friends, but Danny had just whisked me off to dance, saying, 'Thank you.'

Larrisa and Christina had turned up a bit late. It was Christina crying. Yes, she had had another argument with her boyfriend. Oh, it was his fault. She didn't cry for long, though. Ten minutes sobbing in the toilets then we all went back to dancing. I don't think them two left the dance floor all night. Oh, it had been a great night.

Ben had been drunk. He kept telling me he loved me. 'You're so good with Kat, I love that. I love you, Case. You are family. You are Kat's family, so you are our family. We love you, Casey, we really do.' I'd never seen Ben that drunk; it was funny.

Ben's mum had whipped her shoes off and started bumping and grinding to *Dirty* by Christina Aguilera! Oh, my days, I'd almost forgotten that. His dad fell asleep at the table. Oh, it was such a great wedding. We were all hammered. How did I even manage to get up to my own room?

How did I, though? I really couldn't remember. I remembered dancing and stumbling into Danny. We were laughing, and he helped me take my heels off because my feet were hurting. There was a moment. A little moment when I thought we would kiss. We didn't, though, not then. But we did kiss. A flash of us kissing. Where? Did anybody see? Try and think, Casey; you were laughing and joking with him.

Kat and Ben said their goodnights and went up to their bridal suite. I was holding my key card, waving it in front of my face. It was when I was talking to Danny. Why was I holding my card? My mind was blank. I had slid it across the table. Oh my God, I gave it to him. I actually invited Danny up to my room. Why can't I remember properly?

Things started coming back to me. Getting in the elevator alone, the doors starting to close and Danny stopping them. Him coming in. It started there. He kissed me. We kissed each other. His hands were everywhere. We barely got into the room before we started undressing each other. This was the moment we had both been planning for months and months. I could remember it all so clearly now. He kissed me everywhere. All over, every inch of my body. My skin was on fire. Every part of me a hot point. I had never felt this alive. He made me tremble and shiver over and over again, just with his hands and mouth. It was like one continuous orgasm. I wanted him so badly.

I dragged his face up to mine. 'Fuck me.' It was barely a whisper. As he entered me, I instantly came – hard, and without any warning. He stared into my face as I did. 'You are so fucking sexy, you know that?'

I had never had an orgasm through penetrative sex, and somehow with Danny I had them one after the other. Each one crept up on me as a shock. I scratched my nails down his back, and as I did I suddenly felt panicked that I might leave a mark. Oh no, there she was. Erica. The reminder was vivid in my head. What we were doing was wrong. Is that why it felt so good? He had to really feel this. I wasn't imagining. This couldn't be just sex.

He had such longing in his eyes, such passion in his kiss. We had both wanted this for so long. We tried many different positions – some I'd never done before; some I'd never even heard of before. Somewhere around 5am, we both came simultaneously and crashed down onto the bed, breathing heavily.

'That,' he said, between deep breaths, 'was amazing.'

'Yeah.' I was still panting. 'Well worth the wait.'

He covered us both with the duvet, cuddled up to me, and kissed me on the shoulder. 'More than worth it.'

I don't know when we finally fell asleep, but now I was lying in my bed remembering it. I turned my head and saw him there, sleeping next to me. I felt amazing. He stirred a bit.

'Morning,' he said, shuffling back over and throwing his arm around me. 'What time is it?'

I glanced at the clock. 'Ten.'

'I have to go soon.'

My smile faded. Was he going back to her? Was she coming home today? I realised what I had done. I had just had the best sex of my life with somebody else's boyfriend. I was that person. I had become the other woman. The guilt swarmed over me, and I started to feel sick. What had I done? Who was I? I didn't even recognise myself any more.

Chapter Twenty-Five

'Married sex is so much better than engaged sex,' Kat boasted at breakfast, as Ben and Derek went up for seconds of the all-you-can-eat. Katherine disagreed.

'Drunk sex is better than any sex,' she corrected. 'Wait til tomorrow, when you stop being a bride or a new wife, and realise you're now stuck having the same sex with the same man for the rest of his life.' She bit into her toast. 'Obviously, the men tend to die first; hopefully, when we're young enough to jump onto somebody else.' Katherine and her husband were hilarious. They never said a nice thing about each other. Anybody that didn't know them would think they were on the edge of a divorce. Seeing them last night, cheek-to-cheek on the dance floor, it was obvious they were each other's world. Their pet names for each other were wanker and bitch, but they were very much in love.

Kat sat staring at her breakfast sadly. 'Oh my God! I'm not a bride. Oh shit, I'm actually a wife. I wish I could wear my wedding dress every day!'

'Well done, Katherine, you've managed to depress Kat.'

'What about you, missy? Didn't you have a guest in your room last night?'

'What? No? Why would I?' I said very defensively. Danny had snuck out to get back to the bar. What if she had seen us? The part before we went upstairs was still a bit hazy.

'Oh Casey, I'm disappointed with you. That poor guy was here doing you two a favour. The least you could have done was offer him the sofa in your suit.'

'Oh, did poor Danny have to go all the way back to Brighton last night? Bless him. I'll message him and apologise.' She got out her phone.

I relaxed. 'Oh, I did offer, but he just wanted to get back, that's all,' I lied.

I had never lied to my best friend before. I had always been able to tell Kat everything. I told her when I got caught shoplifting at fourteen. I told her when a boy at school got a bit too heavy-handed when we were drunk at the pier. I told her before Max, the last few times I had found out I was pregnant. I could even be honest with her when she was wearing clothes that made her bum look big.

This, I could not tell her. I just couldn't. I checked my phone, but he hadn't messaged. I suppose he didn't have to. I'd seen him this morning, after all. He would be busy at the bar. Who knows what mess his staff would have left it in?

Kat's phone bleeped, and she read it. 'Ahh, bless him. He said he was fine. Best night ever. Isn't that cute?'

Best night ever. That was some compliment. It's nice that he told Kat that and not me. Then again, he would be at his phone now, so I was certain I would get a message off him at some point. Yet hours passed… and nothing.

I didn't hear from Danny for another few days. Every day, I checked my phone… but nothing. I went on Facebook. He hadn't had any posts on his since the day before the wedding. My nosiness took over. I searched through his friends for Erica. I couldn't find her. Her name wasn't on his friends. I figured she had probably just gone off Facebook for a little while. She had done that before. Social media detox.

I typed her name into the search bar and noticed her profile picture flash up – her draped on a flash car, legs up to her armpits.

'What are you doing?' Larissa appeared beside me on her wheelie office chair.

'Shit, you made me jump. Erm, nothing much.'

'Who the fuck is Erica Walker, and why are you Facebook stalking her?'

'She's nobody.' I tried to refresh my page to my home page by pressing back, but it put me onto Danny's page.

'Oooh, who's he?' She leaned over to get a closer look.

'Isn't that the guy from the wedding you kept flirting

with?' Christina had appeared behind me.

'Oh, yes he is. Casey Turner, I believe you have gossip for us.'

'Did somebody say gossip?' Our other colleague Grace shouted from the opposite side of the desk. 'Come on, ladies, spill. Don't disappoint me. I need to know something now.'

I looked round at their three expectant faces, then continued looking and saw all the other faces in the office. 'Fine, there is gossip, but not here.'

'Lunch date in the car park,' Grace called out. 'Looking forward to it.'

The four of us crammed into Grace's 4x4. 'McDonald's? KFC? Which drive-through are we heading to?'

'Don't care.' That was Christina. 'Spill it, Turner. Who is the guy, and what have you done with him?'

'Don't judge me.' I leant forward in my seat straining against my seat belt. 'It's a long story. His name is Danny. He's a friend of my ex's, Max. That girl is his girlfriend.'

'Wow, well done, Danny, bagging a girl like her,' Larissa interrupted.

'She's a bitch. We don't like her.'

'Noted.' She saluted me from the front passenger seat.

'Well, after me and Max, Danny started messaging me. Saying things.'

'Like what?' Grace asked eagerly, signalling into the KFC drive-through.

'Like, he likes me.'

'Go, Casey! Whoop, whoop, whoop!' cheered Christina. 'Casey's gonna get cock.'

I slowly turned my head and looked at her with a worried look on my face.

The drive-through blurted out: *Good afternoon, what is your order?*

'Oh my God! Casey's had cock,' Christina shouted out. All eyes turned to me, wide and waiting for some more information.

'No, we sell chicken.' The drive-through attendant must have heard the last part.

We all burst out laughing, ordered a family bucket, and sped off with our food. Parking up, I explained what had happened. The wedding, the hotel room. 'I haven't heard from him since. He's regretting it, isn't he? He feels guilty, which he should obviously, but I really like him.'

'He's a fuckboy!' Christina blurted out. 'They all are.'

'I shouldn't have gone there. He has a girlfriend.'

'Oh, that doesn't matter.' Grace had a pretty loose view on monogamy. She had very publicly dated her married boss a few years back, before dumping his arse and swapping jobs. 'Babe, he was going to fuck somebody behind her back. Hey, at least you got yours. At the end of the day, you are single. You haven't actually done anything wrong.'

'You won't believe how good it feels actually saying this out loud. It's been this big secret I've been carrying around like a chain,' I admitted.

'At least he isn't actually married yet. I'm still getting messages from that douche that I met when he was out for his wife's birthday! I can't believe he told me she was his sister, and I believed him.' Larissa picked at the smallest portion of chips.

'How did you find out?' I asked her. This was a story I hadn't heard before.

'He admitted it about a week later. I knew something was wrong when she grabbed him and snogged his face off at the end of the night.'

'Yeah, that would be a sign.' Grace rolled her eyes.

'Well, they could have just been really close.'

We looked at each other and chorused, 'Eewwwwww!'

Grace cleaned off her greasy fingers, got out her phone and said, 'Lunch time selfie.' We all leant in, best pouts on show. 'Now for a smiley one,' I said. 'Say Fuckboys.'

'Fuckboys,' we chorused again.

Grace instantly started using her online editor to make us look amazing; she didn't really do *au naturel*. 'I will bash it up when I've done. We better get back.'

Lunch break was over, and I had finally shared my secret. Somehow, I felt less guilty.

Chapter Twenty-Six

It was almost a week before I heard from Danny. I had really thought I was never going to hear from him again. I had given up on him. But there it was, a message on my laptop screen.

Danny - *Hey, babe. How you doing? I keep thinking about that night. Wanna join me and the gang for my birthday drinks?*

I wanted to play it cool. I wanted to ignore the message for as long as I could, but Danny was actually inviting me out for his birthday. Birthdays are a big deal. Ok, he was probably just inviting me as a friend, as technically that is still what we were, but it meant things hadn't been ruined. He still wanted me involved.

Me - *I think you might be forgetting I wouldn't be very welcome. I'm not exactly Erica's favourite person.*

He was typing. Three little dots moving in a sequence showed that he was. They stopped a few times, and then restarted. He was probably thinking how to word it. Yes, you're right, she hates you and now we've slept together I'm not that keen either, so don't bother. The reply I received knocked me sideways.

Danny - *What's it got to do with her?*

What's it got to do with her? It's her boyfriend's birthday! It has everything to do with her.

Me - *Erm... she's your girlfriend!*

Danny - *I don't have a girlfriend.*

I thought I was imagining what I was reading. Danny was single! I remembered the fact they weren't friends on Facebook any more. It could have been a lie, but then they would still be an item on Facebook. He could easily lie to me, but would have a hard time explaining that to her.

Me - *Since when?*
Danny - *Saturday*
Me - *But Kat's wedding was Saturday*
Danny - *I know*

When did they split up? Was it after? No, because he left me on Sunday. Maybe it was before. I thought about when Kat had asked him about Erica. The way he looked away, the fact he said a big 'erm' before it. He had been planning his answer. I had assumed he felt awkward talking about her in front of me, but maybe she wasn't in Milan. Perhaps Danny just didn't want to tell Kat they had split so she didn't feel sorry for him on her wedding day. But he could have told me.

Me - *Does that mean when we slept together you weren't with her?*

Danny - *Correct*

He did a wink smiley face. I had been feeling guilty all this time and we hadn't actually done anything wrong. I spouted that out in a message. I could picture Danny laughing the other side of his screen.

Danny - *Well, you said I wouldn't be able to cheat on her, but you would probably cave in. I was testing the theory. You're a bad girl, Casey Turner. Very bad. I like it.*

What was it about him that made me want to break the rules? Why did I crave him so much? Were Danny and I destined to be together? Two broken halves could make a whole. We messaged for an hour about life in general, spoke about our pasts. In my head, I was planning our future. Erica was out of the picture. Danny could finally be mine.

Danny and I were great together in bed. That first time had been amazing, but every time after that it had got better, and better, and better.

We started to see each other at least once a week. I never thought I liked the term Friends with Benefits, but I was definitely benefiting from that arrangement. We wanted each other anywhere and everywhere. At mine, at his, down alleyways, club toilets. Whenever we got the chance, we were at it. I had got to the point where I thought, *Max who?*

Living so far apart, though, we didn't see each other

enough to become an actual couple. Anyway, he had only just split up from a long-term relationship, so he deserved some breathing space. We spent every other weekend together, sometimes every weekend, and he tended to pop over on Wednesdays as he always had cover at the bar.

I sometimes bunked off and spent the day over there. It was like I was a teenager who had had sex for the first time and just discovered how amazing it was.

Kat got back from a late honeymoon in Barbados, and I couldn't wait to fill her in about it all. Obviously, I missed out the part where I had thought I was a cheating whore.

'Are you two getting together then?' She had a huge smile on her face.

'Not yet. Poor guy has just been released into the single world. If we got together straight away, it wouldn't be fair. He needs his space. I'm trying to stay away from him as much as I can. I don't want to just be his rebound.'

'No way could you be a rebound. You guys have history.'

I finally told her about him admitting that he had liked me a long time ago, without managing to get myself into trouble.

'I know, Kat, but I just don't want our relationship to start with all the ugliness of a break-up attached. I really want to start fresh when he's over it. He needs to spend nights out with the boys. He probably needs to screw a couple of slappers. If we rush straight into it, then a couple months down the line he will feel he's had no chance for any fun. I need to step back and let him have that.'

'God! You're so much better than me. I would be locking him in before he found someone else.'

'You said it yourself, hun, we have history. If you love somebody, let them go and all that.'

My phone started ringing. It was Danny. He invited me to London for the weekend; fancy hotel, a show. He had to check out an old friend's new bar. I didn't hesitate to say yes.

'See?' I placed my phone back in my bag. 'He's already taking me away for the weekend. Another month or two and he's mine.'

Chapter Twenty-Seven

For almost nine months, Danny and I were friends with extras, or seeing each other, or whatever it was you would call it. He had slept with a few other women in that time; I'd had a couple of casual flings with other guys. We always practised safe sex. I'd met his friends; he'd spent time with mine. Everybody commented about how good we were together. It was time to start bringing up the idea of going steady. He had told me he was done with sleeping around. Maybe this was time for us to actually get together.

It was my cousin Becky's birthday, and I was travelling up north to visit her. As I packed my bag into the boot of my car, Danny rang me. 'Fancy some company?'

'What do you mean?' I struggled to put my bag in the boot with the phone clamped between my shoulder and my ear.

'I've cleared my weekend. What do you think about me coming up to your cousin's with you?' I could hear the sound of the bar in the background.

'Oh Danny, you want to meet the family. Do you think we are ready for that?' I joked.

'Family love me. I'm just about to go upstairs and pack my overnight bag, a tee-shirt, boxers, pair of jeans. and about a million condoms. Pick me up on the way.'

Becky was a wonderful woman. I loved her to bits. but she was rather loud. I have always liked to drink, but Becky has wine running through her body like the rest of us have blood. Her house was a madhouse; always people popping in, kids running wild. Every night was a party. This night was extra special because not only was it her birthday, but she hadn't seen me in months. She also had somebody new in her house and she liked to show off a little.

It was all good. I had warned Danny what she was like, but I didn't apologise for it. Becky and I had been close since we were tiny, but her mum moved her up north when she was eleven. We tried to see each other every few months, but it had been almost a year this time.

The music was blaring in her kitchen; we had settled her and her friend's kids in the living room with a million chicken nuggets, a field of chips, and a Disney film on the TV. They couldn't hear the words over the music, but I knew for a fact they had watched this film so many times they probably didn't need to listen to it any more.

Becky's husband Andy sat on the worktop next to a slightly opened window, smoking, beer in hand. He liked to sit back and watch. When he did speak, he normally just told people who he didn't like very much that he really liked them. Danny didn't know this. When Andy was shaking his hand saying, 'I really like you mate', Danny took it as a compliment. I knew that what Andy was really thinking was, 'What is this idiot doing in my house?'

'This is my jam!' Becky suddenly squealed, as a Spice Girls song blared through the speakers. The two of us automatically jumped up and started singing and dancing away, wine glasses in hand. Empty shot glasses and half drunken bottles decorated her usually pristine worktop. There were six of us squashed into their tiny kitchen – we four, plus Andy's friend, Billy and his on-again off-again girlfriend, Kerry. As soon as I'd told Becks that Danny owned a bar, she was all pally with him, inviting herself down for a visit soon.

Becky had her niece Emma over for the evening, paying her for babysitting duties, so we could pop out if we wanted to – or mainly so that somebody sensible was there to watch the kids. Kerry's three children were sleeping over with Becky's four, and Emma had brought a friend with her to help and to keep her company.

We didn't end up going out, and after the children went up to bed the real party started. Danny and the guys popped out to the local shop to get some more wine, as we were running out. We knew they would end up in the pub on the way back, so we didn't expect them home until closing time. We sat on the floor, wine glasses between our legs, doing what girls do best – talking. Hours felt like minutes as we covered all bases of conversation, but it soon turned to Danny and me.

'So, spill the beans, cuz.' Becky lit yet another cigarette. 'What's going on with you guys?'

'We're just friends.'

'Oh hunny, I saw the way he looks at you. You're way more than friends,' Kerry slurred. 'You've either done it, are doing it, or are about to.'

Becky passed her the cigarette. I fiddled with the rim of my glass.

'We've been kind-of seeing each other for a little while now,' I admitted. 'Just, neither of us is ready for anything serious yet.'

I lied again. I wanted serious. This lying in limbo was killing me.

Shouting from outside distracted us. Men's voices sounded loud and angry. I recognised the commotion. It had happened here many times before when I had visited.

Becky ran to the front door. The voices got louder. Billy and Andy were having a showdown in the street. Every time they had too much to drink, they turned on each other. Becky was trying to calm Andy down; once he had reached top gear, there was no bringing him back, but she gave twice as much as he did. Poor Danny had stepped in, pushing Billy back. He was used to sorting out drunks fighting, but normally he hadn't had a skinful himself.

Becky pushed Andy hard. 'Fucking pack it in, you dick. Stop acting the big'un.'

Kerry crossed her arms and rolled her eyes. 'They do this every time. Like dealing with children.'

I had to agree. Poor Becky looked after their four kids basically on her own full time, while he spent his time down the pub or round at his overbearing parents. Evenings were meant to be hers, and you would think Andy would step up a little. This was her birthday, after all. I really did feel for the girl. She never seemed to get a break. No wonder she drank

114

pretty much every day. She just wanted a little escape.

The creak of the stairs gave away that two of the older children had snuck down, hearing what was happening downstairs. Sadly, they were used to their dad's behaviour.

The guys started to calm down after Becky slapped Andy square around the face and threatened Billy she was going to give him the exact same treatment if he didn't wind his neck in. As we walked back into the house, Becky screamed out to a neighbour's house, 'What the fuck are you looking at?'

Mrs. Dobbs from next door shuffled her curtains shut.

Danny breathed a sigh of relief as he passed me in the doorway. I don't think he had packed his bouncer head for the journey. I mouthed sorry at him and he leant forward and kissed me. 'Don't worry.'

The arguing was continuing in the kitchen. Billy was out of the firing line now. Becky was tearing Andy a new one. Danny spotted the kids sitting on the stairs.

'Come on, girls, let's go and find a DVD to watch.' He looked back at me as they climbed the stairs; they looked anxious about what was going on with their mum and dad. 'They shouldn't be seeing this,' Danny muttered to me. 'You go play referee!'

By the time I got into the kitchen, Andy and Becky had gone from arguing to messing about. He had her in a loose headlock, and she was too busy laughing to get out of it. 'I'm going to wet my knickers,' she giggled.

He loosened his grip and hugged her really hard. 'I fucking love you.'

She rolled her eyes at me. We all knew he did. I always felt she was just waiting to see if anyone better came along. They'd been together so long, and unfortunately their mental age had grown worlds apart. She had chucked him out a few times in the past, but the loneliness always got to her. She would rather be in a crappy relationship than on her own. I sighed at how sad that was.

Billy was slouched on top of one of the worktops, when suddenly he turned his attention to me. 'Oi, where's that guy? Who the fuck is he, anyway?'

I explained that Danny had taken the kids upstairs. With that, he appeared in the doorway.

'You, come here, brother.' Billy was a scary guy on the outside. Anybody who didn't know him would run away if he confronted them. Danny had no choice but to stand there. Billy jumped down from the counter and was in his face before anybody could do anything, 'You better be treating her right, boy. I'm telling you that for nothing.'

'Shut up, Billy.' I moved to stand in between them. 'Danny and I are just friends. He doesn't need to treat me any way.'

I remembered Billy doing the same thing to Ben when Kat and I had come to visit. I had really hoped he wouldn't be around this time. No such luck.

He pushed me aside. 'Nothing to do with you, girl. I'm talking to him.' He was back in Danny's face.

'I do, I do. Come on, Bill, she's a really good friend to me.'

Billy stared at him, probably waiting to see a reaction.

'Chill your passion, Billy mate. Calm down.' Andy came over and put his hand on Danny's shoulder, 'See, I like you, mate. I really like you. The first thing I thought when I saw you was, I really like that guy.'

I saw this as a sign it was time to leave. Getting Auntie Denise's spare key and saying our goodbyes, we left the mad house and went two roads down to the quiet empty house. I was relieved my aunt had offered it to us because she was going to be away for her daughter's birthday. Sometimes it was nice to be able to leave Becky's house when things got tense, but it was also quite nice to have Danny to myself for a while.

Chapter Twenty-Eight

After an eventful, but amazing weekend at Becky's, I didn't see Danny for quite a while. We were both really busy. We didn't even talk that often. In fact, thinking about it, we hadn't talked at all. We had had a lovely couple of days there, after that night. Everything had been ok when the drink wasn't flowing. We had laughed about the events, and he told me it was so nice I had people that cared about me that much.

I got on with my life. I had already agreed to give Danny space, so I was cool with this arrangement. Well... I was for the first week and a half. Then I got a bit confused. Why wasn't he getting in touch? I had heard from him, but I had always been the one who messaged first. My *'hey, u ok?'* was always answered by *'yeah, you?'*

When I told him Kat was pregnant, he replied saying, 'Wow'. He would have known that was hard for me, but he didn't ask if I was feeling ok or anything. Danny could be self-centred, but this was odd even for his standards. After about four months of almost total silence, I decided to ask him outright.

Me - *Are you seeing somebody?*

He didn't reply straight away. The tiny picture of him next to my message gave away he had read it, but it wasn't until late the following evening that he eventually replied. I saw that three-letter word I had been dreading.

Danny - *Yes x*

I didn't ask details. I didn't want to know. I cried and called Kat. I had a lovely evening at hers, but her just watching me drink wasn't quite the same. Still feeling low, I called Becky and cried down the phone at her. She had her own drama going on, and we ended up talking about Andy getting arrested and her five-year-old getting in trouble for calling his friend a dickhead at school.

Christina made it clear how angry she was with him, Larissa said I should have it out with him, but I knew it was entirely my own fault. I had played it so cool about the fact we were just friends. I had told him so many times his friendship was important to me. What had I done? I'd given him so much space he'd filled in the gaps with somebody else.

Gradually Kat's belly started to expand, and my job as the excited auntie was getting harder. Don't get me wrong, I was over the moon for Kat, but I could have been married to Max and mum to a ten-year-old by now, worrying about SATs results and secondary school choices. Instead, I was single, and everyone around me was going forwards.

I felt like someone was pressing pause on my life. I threw Kat a baby shower. It was nothing like her cousin's. There were no giant bottles made out of tissue. This was a classy event, catered with everything Kat would have wanted, and alcohol for me. I drank a lot more than I should have – or had planned to – but Becky had come down for it, so throwing down a few glasses of bubbly was easy, even if we were getting glares from some of Kat's more conservative friends. Sneaking a bottle of prosecco under her coat, we went outside so Becky could have a fag. She wasn't her usual self. 'What's wrong with you tonight?'

'Oh babe, my marriage is over. I've told him to get out.'

'Really? Oh hun, you should have said.' I should have guessed. Her three-page Facebook rants never really gave the full story, but enough that I could tell things were not great between them. He wasn't on Facebook, so I was used to her calling him every name under the sun on there.

'He's got this weekend at home with the kids, and then he's gone. I've had enough, Case. I'm done.'

We were sitting outside a bar in Brighton, looking out onto a busy street. I had hired a Hummer limo to drive us from Eastbourne. Kat kept saying it was the best shower she'd ever been to, much to Laura's dismay.

Suddenly, I saw a slim figure walking along the street

ahead of us. She strutted past, head up in the air. Loving herself as usual, I thought. It was Erica. She looked really annoyed, and spun to look behind her and screamed, 'Hurry up, we haven't got all night!'

'I'm coming, I'm coming,' a familiar voice floated on the air, and I went cold. Why was Danny with Erica? As he ran to catch her up and came into view, Becky recognised him.

'Hey, ain't that your mate? Hey, Danny! Alright, babe?'

He paused in front of us like a deer in the headlights. 'Oh, hiya.'

'So good to see ya, babe, give us a kiss.' Becky grabbed him with her cigarette hand and planted a smooch on his cheek, branding him with hot pink lipstick.

Erica huffed in the background and didn't bother to come over. Not that I wanted her nearer to me. I was devastated. He wasn't seeing somebody. He was back with his girlfriend. With her.

He turned to look at me and said, 'Good to see you.'

I couldn't talk. My mouth was open, and I could feel tears prickling my eyes. I nodded.

He pointed towards Erica. 'I better…'

I managed a weak, 'Bye.'

'Aww, it's nice to see him. Who's that with him?'

'I want to go home.' I ran inside before the tears took over.

Feeling sad and really alone, I sat in the corner. All the conversations were about personal stitches and after-birth. I was one of only three people there that hadn't had a baby. Caitlin, Kat's younger cousin, had just got engaged, and Marilyn, the Saturday girl from her work, was only just going off to University and was worried it could affect her relationship with her boyfriend of five months.

Becky was sharing her horrid labour stories with a few other women, and by horror I mean that the baby had come a day too early, so she hadn't had her spray tan or her eyelashes done yet. 'Oh no, love,' I heard her say, 'nobody likes a hairy minge. I don't care how pregnant you are. There is no excuse.'

Kat kept crying. It was the hormones, she said. Her mum was so excited about being a grandma. Ben's mum was excited about finally having a baby boy in the family, as her other son had given her three girls and she couldn't cope with the bickering any more.

I couldn't get the fact that Danny was back with Erica out of my mind. Who could I talk to about it? I decided the only person I wanted to talk to was him. I sat at the bar and tried focussing clearly on my phone, looking for his number. It rang once before it cut off to answerphone. I thought he had probably cancelled my call, as I had forgotten he was with her.

'Hello, Mr Danny. Sorry I didn't talk much when I saw you earlier, but I was a little confused,' I said. Some strange laugh crept out of my throat. I probably sounded insane. 'Now, I know we are just friends. Good friends. Fucking friends. Well, we were. But then we spend this great time together. So great. The way you were with my cousin's kids was amazing – you're really good with kids, by the way. But then I don't hear hardly anything from you, and then I see you with… Well, what do you even want me to say? I see you with that. It. After everything you said about her. Why?' I could feel tears coming again. 'Why didn't you tell me? Why didn't you want…'

I stopped myself. I was drunk. I had to remember that he saw us as fuck-buddies and nothing more. 'Anyway, I'm sorry, I'm really drunk. It's Kat's baby shower. She's going to be a mum.' I instantly cried again. 'I want to be a mum. Danny, I miss you. I miss talking to you every day. You told Billy when we were at Becky's that I was important to you.' My sadness made way for anger. 'Well, maybe it's time you showed it, unless you only said that so you could fuck me. All you guys are the same.'

Making sure I had ended the call, I looked at the barman who was watching me weirdly. 'What? Haven't you seen a drunken stupid woman ranting on the phone to some poor dickhead's answerphone who is completely oblivious to her feelings and is back with his ex-fucking-girlfriend?'

As he slowly shook his head, it suddenly hit me what had I done. I had just left the cringiest message on Danny's machine. How could I get it back?

Chapter Twenty-Nine

My mother's place in New York was stunning. I had only seen these kinds of houses on programmes like *Cribs* on MTV. I didn't think people actually lived in them. I knew Jonathan had money, but wow! It was perfect timing when I got the invite. A good excuse to get away from everything for a while. Kat had random members of her family visiting pretty much from now until the birth, and then probably after, so I knew she would be okay without me for a few days.

I loved the sights of New York. The buzz of the busy streets. People from all walks of life knocking shoulders and clambering past each other. Most people were in a rush; some were meandering slowly, stopping to take photographs of Times Square and the Empire State Building. A ferry ride to get a glimpse of the Statue of Liberty. All the things we had seen hundreds of times in pictures, all looked so much bigger and better in real life.

The food was amazing, too. On my second day, I discovered an Italian restaurant just off Times Square, and I hardly ate anything else when I was sight-seeing. There were also breakfasts so big they filled you up for the rest of the day. If I had been staying for more than a week, I would have ended up the size of a house.

I did most of the touristy bits alone. Mum wasn't the best tour guide. She had been here, seen it, and done it for so many years now that she got bored easily. She had shown me around before, so she reckoned I should know it all. I knew if I had brought some friends with me, she would have started showing off and sharing her wealth of knowledge with us all. My mother did love an audience.

One morning, I was flicking through a magazine while

eating breakfast. Mum's husband Jonathan's face grinned at me across the table. He was so proud of my mum and the things she had done in her life. In his eyes, she could do no wrong. He was a lovely guy, but a million miles away from my dad.

I turned to a page of ads, and there was Erica's pointy face staring back at me. I imagined her gloating and speaking to me, 'Danny is mine and there is nothing you can do to change that.' I slammed the magazine shut and started ranting at Jonathan about my mother, how she invited me over then acted as if I was in the way.

He tried to change the conversation by telling me about the latest awards they had both won in the world of musical theatre. Jonathan loved a name-drop. Andrew Lloyd-Webber this, and Alfie Boe that. There were a few pictures on the wall of my mum and him with different people they had worked with. Not as many as I remembered from before.

Slightly annoyed that he hadn't joined in slagging my mother as the selfish cow she was, I interrupted him talking about the night they had filmed *Les Miserables* at the Royal Albert Hall and how they had met Colm Wilkinson backstage afterwards.

'Hey, Jon.' I knew he hated being called Jon. 'Where are all the other pictures? I'm used to you guys having a gallery in the living room.'

'Oh.' He chewed his crumpet – he had begged me to bring some over for him. 'They are in the achievements room.'

'The achievements room?' I marvelled. Only my mother would have a whole room to brag about what she's done.

'Yeah. It was your mum's idea. She had a lot of stuff to display. I reckon you should check it out before you go home.'

I pulled a face. 'I'm ok, thanks.'

'I really think you should. You might be surprised. It's the door next to my office.'

Loading my empty plate into the dishwasher and finishing my orange juice, I shrugged. Why would I want another reminder of how much better she was than everybody else?

'I'm going to take a shower and get ready to meet Lexi.'

Climbing the stairs, I could hear Mum doing warm-up exercises behind the closed door of her studio. I had chosen to use bathroom number three; it was a wet room – something I'd always wanted.

Only two doors away was Jonathan's office, so I guessed the door with the star on it was what he was talking about. Curiosity got the better of me. Would a small peek hurt?

Pushing down the gold handle and slowly opening the door, I walked into a generous sized, brightly lit room. Pictures lined the two smaller walls, each with their own lighting source. Shelving units with trophies stood proudly in the centre of the room; mannequins with some of Mother's famous costumes decorated the corners. I had seen all these before. Not in quite as grand a manner, but none of it was a surprise to me. I wondered why Jonathan had even mentioned it.

Then my eyes fell on the largest wall in the room. This wall was different. Again, the pictures that lined the walls, I had seen before. The brightly coloured swirls and dots. Animal faces, and people alongside flowers and rainbows. These were not photographs. They were paintings. Drawings in crayons and pencil; a few just rough smudges with charcoal. Each one with a name at the top, written in child's scrawl. Casey. Every single picture I had ever given her was displayed on this wall. A few of my poems in frames. My graduation photo. Everything I had ever done and ever achieved had pride of place in my mother's special room. It was almost like a shrine.

Alongside it, there were pictures of me in ballet and tap classes, certificates from school; a small cabinet housed my first outfits and tiny shoes. There was a picture of me and my mum when I was about six. I was looking at the camera, and she was looking at me. I couldn't remember seeing that look on her face ever. It was the look of pure love. Postcards and letters which I had sent her on her various tours, and on my brief trips away with Dad, were stuck along the centre of the wall.

I heard a noise behind me, and turned to see Jonathan standing in the doorway.

'You have always been your mother's greatest achievement, Casey. I'm just really sorry she's never shown you it.' Then he left, and I heard the door to his office open and shut.

'I can't believe it.' I couldn't stop thinking about that room. 'I always thought I was just a huge inconvenience in her life. Yeah, we sent her pictures all the time, but I always assumed she just threw them away.'

'Oh Casey, don't be silly.' Lexi had been one of the chorus members in Mum's show when I visited when I was eighteen, and we had gotten on really well. We became pen pals and then later Facebook friends, and when she heard I was coming to New York she said we just had to meet up. She had moved onto more TV work than musicals these days, but had just started working with Mum again on *Phantom of the Opera*. 'She is always talking about you. She asks if I've seen your Facebook status, if I've spoken to you. Of course, she loves you. She's your mother.'

We strolled through Central Park, sipping smoothies in plastic cups.

'Think about us poor mere mortals that have to work underneath her. She is this big Broadway star. Nobody cares about little Lexi Cooper when Jill McArthur is in the programme.' She led me to a bench. We had already talked about work and friends and home lives, and I was dreading her bringing up men. I knew it was coming.

'Soooo,' she elongated the word. 'What are you doing here, Case?'

'What do you mean? I'm over to visit Mother. She invited me.'

'She invites you pretty much twice a year, every year. Why now? What's going on?' She knew me too well.

'Erm, nothing.' I fiddled with my straw.

'Why the hesitation?' She put her head down to look at me. 'Awww, hunny. Why so sad? What's he done, and more importantly who is he, and do you want me to kill him? I will, you know, if you need me to.'

I smiled at her. 'It's a very long story. There was a guy,

124

kind of, but he went back.'

'Ahh, there is always a guy. Went back where? Like, to prison?'

'No.' I paused, not really wanting to finish the sentence. 'To his girlfriend.'

'Oh.' She took a long slurp of her drink.

I suddenly noticed a tall guy in sunglasses and a leather jacket, with a group of girls crowded round him. They were throwing notebooks in his face and taking pictures with him. He was signing them, and being pulled in all directions. A large man stood next to him, trying to keep the girls at bay.

'Who's that?' I asked Lexi.

'Oh, that's Mark. He's the new up-and-coming star around here. He's the main guy in a new sitcom.'

'He's fit.' I couldn't help but notice.

'Yeah,' she nodded. 'He's also very taken.' She held up her left hand to show me the rock on her ring finger. I couldn't believe I hadn't noticed it before now.

'Wow, congratulations!'

'I brought him here to meet you. Hey, wait a min.' She ran over to her man, shooing the girls away like a flock of birds surrounding a picnic, before grabbing his hand and dragging him over to me.

'Mark, this is Casey. She's Jill's daughter.'

'Oh wow.' He tilted his hat. What a gentleman. 'How you doing, miss?' He reminded me of Sawyer from *Lost*. He turned to Lexi. 'Is she coming tonight?'

'Oh yes, Casey, you have to. It's the premiere of Mark's pilot, then an after-party. Oh, come on, last time you were over neither of us was legally old enough to drink.'

'Ok, I suppose a première would be fun. What the hell! You only live once, right?'

Premières for TV shows were very different from the ones for films. The head of the TV network had a house so big it made my mum's look like a garden shed.

The cinema room in his basement was impressive. It was a small gathering. A few bigwigs, the cast and some of the crew, a handful of proud mums, wives, and girlfriends… and me.

The show was really good, and I was wondering how long it would be until it was available on our side of the pond.

Mark introduced me to a few of his co-stars. Richard, who played his brother, was twice as handsome as Mark was. Normally, I would have gone weak at the knees, but all I could think about was why Danny had chosen Erica. For the after-party we transferred to a nightclub, where we were all VIPs. I had never been a real VIP before.

Richard didn't really leave my side. He wanted to know how long I was staying in New York, and seemed disappointed when I said I was going home in just two days' time.

'Maybe I can get in touch when I next head to London,' he suggested.

I didn't see the harm in swapping numbers with the guy. It wasn't me, though. TV stars, premières, and VIP areas. But at least it would be a story to tell the girls at work. As nice as New York was, I was ready to go back to my normal and get some routine into my life.

Chapter Thirty

I had never been so happy to walk back through my own front door as I was the evening I got home from New York. I vowed I would someday go over there without Mum knowing I was even in the country. I suppose I didn't really know how to have my mum in my life for more than a day or two at a time. I had just survived seven whole days in her company. I had been unlucky enough to meet her mother-in-law during my visit, too.

The taxi driver, John, helped me in with my cases. He had been a few years above me at school and had become my regular taxi driver since I'd moved back to Eastbourne. I had paid the fare in advance, so I fished in my English purse for a good tip.

'Don't you dare,' he said, pushing the money away. 'Give us a ring when you need me again.'

Shutting the door behind me, I took a slow deep breath in and out. At last, I was in a building with no-one else around. Nobody was going to walk into my bedroom in the morning to rifle through the spare wardrobe for her Gucci-whatever she may or may not have left in there, when she knows you are completely naked.

'Don't be shy, hunny, I made you.' Did that count when she did the same thing and brought her husband in with her?

I was trying to decide between unpacking my case now or diving straight into bed. My bed. I glanced at the clock on the living room wall. It was almost two in the morning, the dirty washing in my bag wasn't going to go anywhere. Bed won.

I had barely walked inside my room when the buzzer went. What had I left in the taxi this time? John had found my purse and passport last time I'd come home from a holiday.

Holding down the intercom button, I said, 'Sorry, John, what have I forgotten this time?'

There was silence for a second. 'Who's John?' a quiet voice crackled through the speaker.

I jumped at the unexpected voice. I tried to speak, but I wasn't really sure what I wanted to say. I had obviously been quiet for too long, because the voice spoke again.

'Is that why I haven't heard from you? You have a new guy?' Danny sounded a little bit drunk.

I stayed quiet for a while, seeing if he would talk some more. He didn't.

'What do you want, Danny?' My voice was strained. He had sent me a couple of messages whilst I was away, asking how I was, if I wanted to meet up. I hadn't replied. There had been plenty of times he hadn't replied to me since he was back with her, so I wanted to see how he liked being ignored.

'Let me in.'

There was a small part of me that wanted to press the door release, throw the front door open, and wait for him naked at the top of the stairs. I obviously wasn't going to do that, though.

'Where's Erica?' I asked, clearing my throat first.

He paused. His voice was quieter this time. 'At home.'

'Why aren't you there?'

'I wanted to see you, Casey. I miss you. Let me in.'

After a few more minutes considering the options, I realised I was going to let him in no matter what the outcome. It was Danny. How was I going to send him away? He had a girlfriend again though now, so things were going to be different. We would have to go backwards and learn how to be friends all over again.

Danny had other ideas. I opened the door as Danny reached the top of the stairs, and before I knew what was going on his lips were on mine and I was pushed up against the wall.

'Danny, what are you doing?' I tried to push him away, but it felt so good kissing him again.

'I'm gonna take you to bed and kiss you everywhere, before sliding inside you and giving you a night you'll never forget.'

'What about Erica?'

He covered my mouth. 'Shh, we don't need to talk about her.'

One side of me wanted to scream at him, push him away, and throw him out. How dare he! That was a disgusting way to treat somebody he was supposed to love. I also knew I deserved better than being his dirty secret, no matter how much it sometimes appealed to me.

The other side of me was enjoying this far too much to care. The smell of him, the taste. I felt like I had come home. As the two sides of my brain fought each other, I stopped thinking about anything and let him carry me through to my bedroom.

Straight after we'd made love, he jumped up and started getting dressed. The reality of what had happened was playing on my conscience. The relief I had felt when I found out he hadn't cheated the first time round made this guilt feel twice as strong.

I watched him storming round my room, picking up discarded items of clothes. 'Where's my phone?' he was muttering under his breath. Finding it under his jacket, he looked up at me and smiled. 'Are you ok?'

I wasn't sure if I was, but I nodded anyway. He normally stayed. He would normally be snoring at my side now or cuddled up, talking about his day. This was the difference. If I was willing to date a man who had a girlfriend, I would have to deal with stolen moments and short encounters.

He climbed over my bed to lay on top of me and kiss me goodbye. My completely naked body was separated from his by a duvet, his clothes, and a million miles.

'See you soon.' He grabbed his coat and left.

I told myself I had to remember this feeling. I hoped that memory would stop me from ever making this mistake again. I curled myself into a ball and cried myself to sleep.

It didn't stop me, though. The feelings go away, and the memory of multiple orgasms take over. Every message I thought was him, every knock at the door. I started to crave him again. My old way of thinking came back. I didn't owe anything to Erica. If he was sneaking off and she didn't realise why, then it was her own fault.

Kat had given birth to a beautiful baby boy, and even though no blood was shared between us, I fell brilliantly into my proud auntie roll. The second I held her little baby in my arms, every inch of sadness I had about not having my own baby disappeared. Every day I wasn't working, I was at hers, helping with housework and keeping her sane with gossip from the office.

One lunchtime, as Brody slept in my arms, I turned to my best friend in the world and finally told her what I had been trying to hide for so long.

'Kat, please don't judge me.'

'What's wrong, hun?'

'I'm sleeping with Danny still.' No sooner had the words left my lips than I wanted to take them back. I was ready for Kat to scream and shout at me and throw me out of her house, but I knew that I couldn't carry on keeping secrets.

'Isn't Danny back with Erica?' she asked, as if there was nothing wrong with it. I nodded. 'Well, that must me hard. How are you feeling about it?'

'At first, I felt bad. Guilty. Dirty even, but now, I feel great. I have realised that having just some of him is better than having none of him at all.' I wanted her to shout at me, to yell, to start comparing me to the slags that Sean had slept with.

Instead, she just tilted her head to the side. 'Ahh, it's a shame he got back with her. You two were really good together. Oooh, let's watch *Loose Women*, I think Katie Price is on today.' She switched TV channels and went to make us tea.

As she walked back into the room, she continued speaking. 'I'm sure he will see one day, hun. She's horrid to him; we've both seen it. There has to be something wrong with their relationship or he wouldn't still be seeing you. He obviously has some sort of feelings for you.'

I looked down at the sleeping baby in my arms and smiled. 'Yeah, one day he'll see.' I had Kat's approval.

Chapter Thirty-One

A whole year passed, and things hadn't changed. Danny kept appearing at my door without warning. He had bought himself a second bar in Eastbourne and spent half his time there, so we found it easier to see each other. Erica was working away more and more, as her modelling career was taking off. This also meant I saw her face everywhere.

Now, when I saw photos of her, I could talk back to her. *Actually, he's ours. We share him, but one day he's going to be all mine.* I had become proud of being the other woman. I was having all the fun with none of the bullshit. I knew about her, she didn't know about me. If you thought about it, I had the upper hand.

On the four-year anniversary of Nan's death, I went to visit her and Grandad's grave. I hadn't been for a while, and felt awful. As I got there, I saw a familiar figure placing flowers on the ground.

'Max?'

He spun around. 'Hey, Casey. I'm sorry. I hope you don't mind, I just...'

'Of course I don't mind. It's really nice of you to come.'

I hovered a little way away. I was worried if I took a step forward, he would run into the undergrowth like a frightened animal. He looked like he had the weight of the world on his shoulders. I took small steps forward. He moved back a little so I could get in, and I knelt on the ground to start trimming my flowers and arrange them into the plastic vase.

'How have you been?' I asked casually.

He didn't say anything, but with a small glance to my side I noticed he was nodding. 'Good.'

I wanted to fill the silence. 'Coming up to the big four zero

131

this weekend, huh?'

He shuffled awkwardly from foot to foot, both hands planted deep inside his pockets.

'Casey, I was kind of hoping I'd bump into you,' he said. 'I need to speak to you. Do you fancy lunch?'

I didn't see how it could hurt, so I finished fixing the flowers and we arranged where to meet before getting into our separate cars.

The harbour was beautiful on a sunny day. There were lazy seagulls floating on the tranquil water between the rows of boats. Amongst the cluster of restaurants was a favourite of Max's. When we used to do dinner and a movie, he had always opted for the Harvester over all the Italian restaurants and posh fish and chips. We were seated in the corner. It had been our usual table.

When the waitress came over, Max automatically gave our order then looked at me with a horrified look on his face. 'Oh my God, Case, I'm so sorry. You probably—'

I stopped him. 'No, it's fine. My food preferences haven't changed much.' She went off to get our drinks.

'You look good.' Max stared at me for a rather long time.

'You do, too,' I replied politely. He didn't. He looked tired and stressed. 'Why are we here, Max? What do you want to speak to me about?'

He rung his hands together and sighed deeply. I thought the worst. Did he have another cancer scare? Was it more than a scare? He looked back at my face. 'I really wanted to be the person to tell you. I didn't want you to hear it from anybody else.'

I reached out to touch his hand. 'Are you sick? Are you ok?'

'I'm fine.' He cupped his hand over mine.

'Is it Lisa? Is she ill?'

'No, she isn't ill. Nobody is.'

I breathed a sigh of relief. Then what was wrong?

'She's pregnant, Case. I'm gonna be a dad.'

'Wow.' I wasn't sure how I felt about this information. I stared down at the empty table before me, bringing my hands out of his and into my lap.

'I'm really sorry.'

My head flung up to face him. 'Don't be silly, Max, it's great news. It really is. You have nothing to be sorry for.'

He leant back in his chair. 'Then why are you crying?'

It was only then that I noticed big blobs of tears running down my face. I wiped them away and changed my crying into laughing. Max laughed, too. I really was happy for him. I was crying for me.

Chapter Thirty-Two

'So, did you tell him about Danny?' Kat quizzed me. It was her first night out since having Brody, and she had been downing drinks like they were going out of fashion. I had only just told her about bumping into Max.

'No.' I was shocked she had even asked that. 'What was I meant to say? Hey, Max, remember your old friend you've known since he was sixteen and you now don't even talk to, I've been screwing him. Behind his girlfriend's back.'

'And he's got a better penis,' she hiccupped.

'Not better, different.'

'And it makes me sing in every way.' She was in her giggly mood. I ordered myself another drink as she carried on giggling about willies.

We were having a great night. Kat hadn't changed. I thought being a mum might have had her yawning in the corner, or checking her watch. Instead, she put her phone in her pocket on vibrate and told me Brody was with his dad, who was more than capable of taking the reins for one night.

I couldn't have been happier, as it had been so long since we had been out together. The conversation steered to Max and Danny a few times during the evening. Near the end of the night, Danny text me.

'He's on his way to mine,' I told Kat. 'Our taxi is due in five minutes.'

'What do you think Max would have said about Danny?' she asked, starting to get her coat on.

'God knows. Maybe he would have offered to join us?' I found this idea hilarious.

Kat didn't. 'Erm, don't forget, Max has a girlfriend.'

'Yeah, so does Danny.' I shrugged. I had only been joking

about the Max thing, but Kat was being deadly serious. I hadn't read the signs, though, and thought she was on the same drunken wavelength as me. 'Besides, he was mine first, for years.'

'Well, in that case, Erica was Danny's first,' she replied.

Ouch, the truth hurts when it's tied to a rock and thrown in your face.

'Ok, best friend, what happened to not judging? You said you were cool with this.'

They say that drink can bring out the truth, and from what came out of Kat's mouth next I knew she had been bottling up her true feelings for a while.

'You can do what you like, Casey, but it doesn't make you look any less of a fool, running home to shag some guy that is never going to be yours. Face it. He got back with her when he didn't need to. Before you know it, he's going to be marrying her and having babies, and you'll be thrown to the gutter and he won't give you a second thought.'

Kat had never spoken to me like that before. I was usually the one with the vicious tongue. But I couldn't answer her. I couldn't argue back. Everything she said was right.

As right as she was, I still wasn't ready to admit it, so I stormed off outside to wait for our taxi. We didn't speak a word the whole way home.

As I got out, I just said, 'Bye' before slamming the door shut. Danny was sitting on the wall by my door.

'Don't talk,' I told him. I was still fuming with Kat. 'Take me upstairs, but I don't want to have to talk. '

What is it about angry sex? I was angry at the world, angry at Kat for making me see the truth, angry at Max for having everything we had ever wanted. Angry at Lisa for being able to give it to him, but most of all I was angry at Danny. I was angry at him for choosing Erica. I was angry at him for using me. I was angry at him for making me fall in love with him.

That anger transpired into the sweatiest, dirtiest, and best sex I had ever had in my life. I was left panting and exhausted, but even after he fell asleep, I couldn't. I lay staring at him. The anger hadn't worn off.

Why was I settling to be second best? He chose her. It came down to the crunch and he chose Erica. He didn't even tell me about it. I obviously didn't even cross his mind. I had been sleeping with him and spending time with him for a whole nine months, and he didn't even consider me when he got back with his girlfriend.

Actions speak louder than words, so no matter how many times I had heard him say to people that I was special and I was important, he had a very funny way of showing it. I kept looking at him. What was so special about this guy in front of me that I had completely changed the way I looked at the world?

It was *not* ok that I was sleeping with him. He had a girlfriend. It didn't matter that I didn't like her. It wasn't moral. It didn't matter that he was willing to cheat. What mattered was I would never have done that before.

All these jumbled thoughts were racing through my head, and anger started rising inside of me. It wasn't ok that he had come between me and my best friend this evening. It wasn't ok that he used to be Max's friend. It wasn't ok that he came away with me for a weekend to see my family and then went quiet. It wasn't ok that he ignored messages I'd sent him for days or even weeks. None of it was ok.

'Get out,' I whispered, staring hard at his sleeping face. 'Get out,' I said a little bit louder. I wanted him to wake up. I needed this over now. 'Get out, get out, get out, get out!' Each word got louder, and I began to push him. I wanted him away from me now.

He woke with a start. 'Woah, what's wrong?'

'Get out!' I was yelling now, bringing the duvet up to cover my naked body. I didn't want him to look at me.

'Babe…'

'Don't you dare call me that. I am not your babe! Get out of my flat. Get out.'

'Case, what's wrong?' He looked bewildered.

'What's wrong? What is wrong? What do you think Danny, you tell me? You tell me what is wrong. In fact, it would be so much easier to ask what is right, because the answer is nothing. Nothing is right about this.'

I got out of bed and started pacing up and down. I was feeling trapped and suffocated, and I needed to be out of this situation.

'Hey, calm down. Let's just get back into bed and talk.'

'No, Danny, I mean it. I need you to get out.'

Danny rubbed his face, probably trying to wake himself up. 'It's four in the morning. Where will I go?'

'Go back to your girlfriend, Danny. Go back to her. That's where you want to be anyway.'

'Case, of course I want to be here.'

I put on an oversized t-shirt, stood up straight and looked right at him. 'Why?' I asked.

He looked confused, but I ploughed on. 'Why Erica? What does she have? What is so special that you chose her?'

'Case…'

'No, Danny, I want to know. You spent months telling me how crap your sex life was, how bad a girlfriend she was, how she is always away. So, why choose her? We were so good together and you chose her.' He stared at me, disbelief on his face. 'You absolute arsehole!' I spat at him.

A sudden surge of anger flashed across his face. 'You knew exactly what you were getting into, Case. You knew I had a girlfriend when we started this.'

A wave of disappointment washed over me as my voice cracked and tears started to roll down my face.

'No, I didn't. Yes, you had a girlfriend when we started talking, but then you split up. I allowed myself to fall for you when you were split from her, then – without any warning at all – you were gone, and she was back in your life and… and… and…' My words started to peter out.

I was sobbing now, and my voice had gone so high-pitched I didn't think he could hear me anyway. He ran round the bed and held me as I sank down onto the floor, pulling me into his arms and onto his lap. He rocked me, shushing me gently, as I cried and held him tightly. I wanted him to go, but when he held me like this I didn't ever want him to leave. He stroked my hair and kept repeating he was sorry.

137

'I love you,' I sobbed.

'I'm sorry, Casey. I really didn't mean to hurt you.'

'Why her?' I asked so quietly that the words nearly didn't come out.

He lifted me up and sat me on the bed. 'We have history, babe. Her and me.' His voice was gentle. 'We've been together for a very long time. I can't see anything bad happen to her.'

I wiped my tears away and looked at him, puzzled. Why would anything bad happen to her? Danny looked sad.

'She hurts herself. Not always, just sometimes. When you and I got back from visiting Becky, she came into my bar with both wrists sliced open. She told me she was going to kill herself if we couldn't be together.'

'But that's no reason to be with someone,' I argued.

'I love her, Casey. I do. In my own way. She isn't easy to love, but I made her a promise and I like to stick to my word.'

'What about me?' I sounded so pathetic.

'I really do care about you. You make things easier for me. You are my escape. I need you both.'

I shook my head. No, I wasn't prepared to feel worthless because I made it easier for this man to cheat on his girlfriend. I looked straight at him and parted my lips. He leant forward to kiss me, but I stopped him.

'So, go.' And I got up and walked out of the bedroom.

I waited until I was in the safety of my living room before I let myself cry again. After a while, I heard the door close quietly, and knew Danny had just walked out of my life for good.

Chapter Thirty-Three

The Oxford English Dictionary defines cheating as to act dishonestly or unfairly in order to gain an advantage. To be sexually unfaithful. I don't know what either of us had gained from the years I wasted on Danny. People said he had used me, but we had used each other. I had been a broken woman and I had let him fix me. Unfortunately, I had also assumed that I couldn't be the new me without him. I was wrong.

Summer arrived, and the days got longer, and life in general felt brighter. I threw myself into work, and with my extra energy being put to better use, I managed to get a promotion in the office. I rang my parents more often. I vowed to never argue with Kat again. I deleted Facebook, and tried living in real life. That only lasted a few days, though. As I said before, I was addicted. I did, however, delete and block all the negative people from my life, starting with Danny.

I celebrated every birthday, anniversary, and wedding that crossed my path, and stopped feeling sorry for myself. That person was gone. I stopped seeing pregnant women as a punishment, but as the joyous thing it was. So, babies might not be in my future, but that didn't mean there was anything wrong with other people making a future for the world. I had options. If I ever did meet the right guy, we could adopt, or foster. I thought about all the abandoned children in the world I could help.

I liked being the cool auntie anyway. Brody was my world. His little face made my heart leap every time I saw it. I didn't get a single pang of jealousy when Kat told me she was expecting again, and in time she had a beautiful baby girl, Alesha.

Everybody I knew was carrying on with life. Becky was

doing so much better after finally kicking Andy out. He had been bringing her down for far too long. After a few months of juggling the kids on her own, she had met a lovely young man. Daniel treated her and the children how they should have been treated all along. It took a while, but Andy eventually stepped up to his role as part-time dad, and all the family were happier for it.

Larissa got married, but decided she wasn't ready to start breeding yet. We all encouraged her to give us a baby to cuddle – even me – but she loved the freedom her partner gave her, and she stayed as my regular drinking buddy after work and weekends.

Christina started putting herself first. She wouldn't let her baby daddy treat her badly, and they became a strong couple. I loved to see her smiling every day instead of coming in almost in tears.

Grace managed to bag herself a dashing young pilot she had been after for years, and gave up our office to join him in the skies. I was glad to be invited to their wedding, but knew I was going to miss seeing her face every day.

Katherine and her husband renewed their wedding vows, with their children as bridesmaids and page boys. It was a beautiful day that didn't coincide with any football match, so everybody had a smile on their face – even Derek.

Max and Lisa had a baby girl. They called her Bethany. I didn't see her, but I saw his mum in town carrying a baby girl balloon and stopped her to chat. I posted them a congratulations card and put a £20 voucher in it for a designer baby clothes shop in Brighton that we used to look at in the early days.

Dad got a girlfriend. I couldn't believe it when he brought her down to see me for a visit. They stayed with George, who lived not far from my flat, and I have never seen my father smile so much. Mum and Jonathan were taking New York by storm, and Lexi and Mark were starring together in a new Quentin Tarantino film.

I heard that Danny got dumped. Erica apparently met somebody else on a photo shoot in Paris, and was now living it up in Milan. She didn't even tell him. Just moved out her stuff when he was at the other bar. I suppose he rather deserved that treatment, but I couldn't help feeling a little bit sorry for him. Not sorry enough to accept the message request I had from him on Messenger.

Looking at my phone, I updated my Facebook status. *Feeling Happy*. I walked round the corner to the shop and could hear updates coming through. A heart from Ben, which gave away that Kat was using the wrong Facebook again.

So glad, commented Katherine.

Keep it up, girl, from Lexi.

I was taking myself out on a date. Nibbles from Asda for during the film, and then maybe some dinner at Frankie and Benny's. Once upon a time the idea of sitting in a restaurant or the cinema on my own would have terrified me. But I was Casey Turner. I could do anything I put my mind to.

Paying for my ticket using my Apple Pay, I felt like someone was watching me. Glancing over, a man with tanned skin and a shaved head was looking my way. He nodded his head at me, and I smiled shyly in reply. My one single ticket felt very light in my hand, and I looked down to switch my phone off and placed it in my bag. When I looked up again, he was gone.

They had let in the crowd for the other screen, so I had either imagined him or he had gone in there. After the movie, I waited until I was sitting comfortably in the restaurant and ordered my drink, before I turned my phone back on. Checking the other comments and reactions on my earlier post and then scanning the menu for what I wanted to eat, I heard a voice close to me.

'Is this seat taken?'

I looked up to see the man from the cinema. Smiling, I shook my head. We ate, drank, and laughed long into the night.

I was never looking for love. It kind of just happened.

Fantastic Books
Great Authors

CROOKED
CAT

Meet our authors and discover
our exciting range:

- Gripping Thrillers
- Cosy Mysteries
- Romantic Chick-Lit
- Fascinating Historicals
- Exciting Fantasy
- Young Adult and Children's
  Adventures
- Non-Fiction

Printed in Great Britain
by Amazon